HIDDEN FILES

True cyber crime investigation stories

Yuvaan
books
An Imprint of Unbound Script

HIDDEN FILES

Written *by* AMIT DUBEY

ISBN : 978-93-48497-22-2

First Edition : October, 2025

Second Edition : July, 2026

Publisher : Unbound Script
2/41, Ansari Road,
Daryaganj, Delhi-110002
Website : www.unboundscript.com
E-mail : books@unboundscript.com
Phone : 011-35807601

Printer : Yash Printographics
Noida, Uttar Pradesh

Price : ₹ 275/-

HIDDEN FILES

True cyber crime investigation stories

AMIT DUBEY
Cyber investigator

To our beloved parents,
whose prayers day and night
make our every attempt a success.

CONTENTS

INTRODUCTION

Nowadays everyone spends a large part of their day online, whether it's shopping, bill payments, making friends, selling cars or buying a house, from college admission to finding a marriage partner, our lives have become totally dependent on our online community. There is a world which is parallel to the real world, which we call the virtual world, but all the crimes that occur in the real world are possible in this virtual world too, so It has become very important to keep ourselves aware of the dark realities of this virtual world.

There is curiosity and eagerness, but in this rushing world we have no time to learn these guidelines. The videos or messages imparting knowledge such as "Don't give OTP, don't click the link or share a detail on the phone" etc seem to be quite boring. When we face a real criminal, we forget such directions because we are trapped in a unique way. I felt that people might forget guidelines but they always remember stories. So why don't I tell these guidelines through stories and that is when I came up with the idea of 'hidden files'.

In fact, I have shared some of our real life experiences through these stories, and as I believe that truth is much more thrilling than fiction. These stories will not only warn you about cyber threats but will also empower you to deal with such criminal cases.

It is my endeavor to make more and more people aware through stories and to protect everyone against the growing dangers of the virtual world.

Amit Dubey

1 THAT GIRL ON THE HIGHWAY

I would love to change the world,
but they won't give me the source code.

It must have been just past 6 in the evening, but being wintertime it had already started to get dark.

The Noida-Greater Noida expressway-the same expressway infamous for road accidents and crimes. On this very expressway, a 20-22 year old beautiful, young woman was walking with quick strides along the highway road. This was definitely not a usual occurrence.

Dark, kohl-rimmed eyes, long hair streaming out behind her, in her pink top and blue designer skirt she was a vision indeed. In one hand she held a longish purse and a mobile phone in her other hand. She glanced at her phone at intervals and would then resume walking.

Fast driven cars would automatically slow down for a fraction of a second when they neared the young woman. The driver inside would be staring hard at her as if to read her expression.

The terrified woman kept looking back every time she heard a car approach; unwittingly she would also glance at the drivers. Sometimes, the drivers smiled.

In this country, it was not at all unusual for a passerby to stare at a woman walking alone on the road. What was unusual however, was the very presence of this young woman on the highway. What was she doing there? How did she get there?

It could be that she had had a spat with her boyfriend or husband and in a huff she may have gotten off the car. But what kind of unfeeling boyfriend or husband must he be, for him to let her be alone on such a dangerous highway?

Or it could be that she may have been on her way home in a taxi and the taxi-driver might have misbehaved with her, forcing her to abandon the taxi and continue on foot.

Whatever the reason for her being there, at 6 pm on this dangerous highway was an extremely unsafe situation for her to be in. A gentleman would never stop on seeing her and a man with unlawful intent would surely stop by her only to commit a crime.

PARP! PARP! Suddenly, another car, honking loudly, drove past her. The driver again, turned to stare hard at her. Maybe he was hoping for some kind of reaction. But the girl turned a deaf ear and a blind eye to him. The driver appeared disappointed; he revved his engine and drove away.

The woman had barely walked a few more steps when another car honking loudly came by. This time around, the driver not only stared hard at her but pulled over really close to her.

"Can I give you a lift to somewhere ma'am?" he asked, a strange smile playing on his face. His words held less of a request and more of an invitation.

The woman glanced at him for a second and resumed walking.

The driver drove his car slowly alongside her walking figure.

"It's late, it is not safe here for you Ma'am," this time the driver tried to sound concerned.

"That is why I am offering you a lift," but his wolfish expression gave him away.

The woman continued walking.

Suddenly, there was a cacophony of horns from behind the driver, this shook him and he hurriedly drove away. The young woman was once again alone, walking along the highway, which was very unsafe at best.

Not very long after, a big vehicle drew up near her and the driver slowed his car to enquire.

"Are you OK Ma'am, is there something wrong?"

the driver pulled up right next to her.

The car appeared to be an Audi Q5, a 24-25 year old good looking young man was behind the wheel. The woman looked him over carefully.

"Thanks, but I'm fine," she replied and then resumed walking.

"Hey, listen, let me drop you at the next stop, you can get a bus from there," the young man again called out to her. "No buses will stop here, in the middle of the highway."

The girl thought for a moment. "OK," she opened the passenger door next to the driver and got in.

"Look here, I have a knife, don't think of me as weak," she said, as soon as she had climbed in.

"Absolutely, with the way things are these days, girls should carry knives with them," the young man replied smiling.

The woman turned to glare at him, trying to appear angry; it only made her appearance even more beautiful. She opened her purse, glanced inside and brought out a clip. She combed back her hair with her fingers and fastened it with the clip. The young man glanced at this move of hers out of the corners of his eyes and remarked.

"Beautiful. You have such beautiful hair," he said hesitantly.

"Hmmm...." the woman glared at him.

"Ajay, my name is Ajay, what's yours" he held out his hand towards her.

"I'm sorry, but I don't tell strangers my name."

"That's ok, after 5 minutes we will no longer be strangers, then you can tell me your name," the young man threw a smile at her.

"Would you mind driving a bit faster," the woman replied scathingly.

"Most accidents on this road happen due to speeding. One never knows when an animal may suddenly appear before your car. You should be grateful that you are with me."

"So, do you live in Greater Noida?" he asked. "Why?"

"Just asking. It's late to take a bus. I could drop you off till your house."

"Look here, you have been kind enough, I can go by myself," she again sounded miffed.

"It looks like you are new here," the man said after an interval.

"Why?"

"Well, if not, you would not dare to be alone this way on this highway."

"Really, so what do you think could happen?"

"Well, a beautiful young woman like you, all alone on the highway, it could easily give someone wrong intentions." Saying this, the young man began laughing loudly.

"Stop the car! Right now! Stop!" the woman scolded him.

"Wh..What happened?" the man could not figure out what was the matter.

"Right now! Stop!" the woman screeched at him.

The man suddenly felt a pistol being driven into his side.

The woman's eyes were red with rage.

"Don't try to act smart, I will blow your brains out."

"I... I'm stopping, one second...," the colour had washed out of the young man's facc.

Veering, he pulled the car up next to a lamp-post. By this time, however, the car had already travelled about 600-700 metres more.

"Get down," the woman screamed at him.

"Ok.. Ok," the man tried to reach for his mobile as he started to open his door.

"Leave your mobile... get out of the car now...," the man climbed out. He was shocked and horrified; he could not make sense of what was happening with him.

The woman quickly slid over to the driver's side and yelled at him, "Go on... get out of here."

"Ma'am you got into my car with the intent of robbing me, but unfortunately for you, you won't be able to get too far with my car."

"Why? Are you low on petrol?" the woman glanced towards the fuel indicator on the dashboard.

"No, but my mobile is in the car. I will soon stop somebody and phone the police and within 2 minutes they will use my phone's location to grab you."

"Oh... In that case, here goes your mobile," she said, throwing the man's mobile out of the car window.

"Actually, just getting rid of my mobile will not help; you will still get caught."

"Don't talk nonsense... I'm leaving...," the woman started the car.

"But listen, for the last 10 minutes your mobile and my mobile have been in exactly the same locations. It won't take the police longer than 10 minutes to figure out whose mobile it was that was changing location at exactly the same time as mine. Once they have your number, they have got you."

"Hmmm... Ok, then I will throw away my mobile too," the woman stuck her hand out to throw out her phone.

"Throwing your phone away will not help. Just think... your phone number is on a server... they will get your mobile number anyway... once they have your number, they can get your AADHAR card details, your address... everything."

"Oh, what do I do then?" the woman appeared a bit worried now. She thought for a moment and then leapt out of the car.

"Look here, I'm going to scream now, people will gather and I will claim that you have been behaving inappropriately with me. They will beat you up and you will be thrown in jail. I will do it, unless, you hand over all the valuables that you have on you right now and then get the hell out of here."

"Ma'am, I'm sorry, but you won't be able to do this either."

"Why not?"

"Look up. I pulled over my car at this particular lamp-post on purpose," the woman glanced up at the lamp-post that he was indicating.

"There is a CCTV camera here which has been recording us for the last 5 minutes. This is proof that I have not behaved with you in any way that you are claiming.... so, the one going to jail will be you... not me."

"Fine, I will break this camera then," the woman replied, looking up at it.

"That won't be of any use, it's an IP camera, its recording has already been uploaded on to a server, breaking the camera will not make any difference."

The young woman was visibly sweating now, in spite of the cold weather. "Look... listen... I'm sorry... Please let's forget this happened."

"You just leave from here and let me be," she folded her palms and literally begged him.

"I'm terribly sorry ma'am but we can't end this like this. I cannot leave you and go away."

"But why? Please, just forgive me, forget whatever happened and let me be," once again the woman implored.

"Look, for the last 15 minutes mine and your mobile locations have been the same, thus proving that we were together. Also, this camera has been recording us for the last 7-8 minutes. Now, if, as you say, I leave you alone and drive away and god for bid something were to happen to you or you do something to hurt yourself; I will unnecessarily get implicated. I will never be able to prove that I was not with you and that I had nothing to do with whatever may happen to you."

"Oh... Ok... then what should we do now?" the woman was close to tears now.

"There's only one way out now."

"What is that?"

"That being, you come with me in my car, I will drive you to your house and meet with your parents, so they can acknowledge that I have, indeed, dropped you home safe and sound."

"Do you mean to say... you are coming home with me? And what am I supposed to tell my parents? How do I explain to them who you are?"

"Well, that's for you to decide, what you want to tell your parents. But there really isn't any other way out of this ma'am," the young man reached in the bushes for his mobile phone as he said this. He retrieved his phone and then jumped back into the driver's seat of his car.

"Alright, let's go then," the woman looked crestfallen. She opened the passenger door and climbed up in, next to him.

Nobody spoke. There was absolute silence now as he drove.

"Well, where do I drive to, at least tell me your address," the young man glanced over at her and enquired.

"Sector Alpha," the woman mumbled and continued staring straight ahead. The young man turned up the volume dial on his car radio. Music from 93.5 Red FM boomed out.

2 A NIGHT WITH ATM ROBBERS

Our freedom can be measured by
the number of things we can walk away from.

Amit was in deep sleep when he was suddenly woken up by the buzzing of his mobile phone.

"Who is it?" he answered the phone without glancing at the screen.

"Sir, this is inspector Yadav. Dilip sir gave me your number. We need your help."

"Isn't it too early to phone," Amit answered irritably.

"Sir, we have been waiting all night for it to be morning before we phoned, it's morning now. Sir, I would be very grateful if you could come over to the Surajpur police-station."

"What has happened?" Amit glanced at the mobile screen to check the time as he asked. It was 7:00 am.

"Sir, somebody has stolen an ATM, last night, around 2 am.

"Hmmm... ok... I'll be there soon."

Amit was just pulling on his shoes when Kumud awoke. "Where are you off to, so early in the morning?" she enquired sleepily.

"Just stepping out for a morning run."

"Well... why do you need your car keys then," Kumud's sharp eyes had noticed Amit reaching for his car keys.

"It's just... the air quality in our society is quite poor so I figured I would drive to Surajpur park for a run," Amit hurriedly left the house before Kumud could question him any further.

Miffed, Kumud pulled a pillow towards her and went back to sleep.

"Where's Dilip," Amit asked as he entered the Surajpur police station.

"Sir, he will be coming in late."

"Then why on earth did you wake me up so early in the morning? His highness will arrive when he feels like while you are leeching the life out of me." Amit grumbled.

"Sir, he instructed us that if we were unable to find a clue in this particular case then we were required to call you in."

"I see, so you don't even have any clues or leads... then what on earth have you people been doing all night?"

"Sir, we only know that the ATM was stolen between 2 and 4 am."

"Excellent work, what a marvellous hint, I think this may just solve the case for us," Amit replied sarcastically.

"Beta sector... this ATM?" Amit pulled up a Google street map on his laptop and indicated towards an ATM icon on it.

"Yes, I think it is this one," the inspector peered into Amit's screen. It was apparent though that he could not make head or tail of what he was being shown.

"Airtel... Idea...Vodafone...," Amit murmured to himself as he worked on his laptop. Certain towers began popping up on the map on his screen.

"Anyone here from the cyber cell?" he inquired.

"Yes, there is someone sir. Dilip sir had instructed us earlier itself to get someone from the cyber cell to assist you," the inspector gestured towards a scrawny youth; he appeared to be around 22-23 years old and sat clutching a laptop to himself.

"Are you from the cyber cell?" Amit asked him.

"Yes sir."

"What's your name?"

"Rajbir, sir."

"When did you join?"

"Two months ago sir."

"Well, what all can you do Rajbir?" Amit asked him.

The youth hesitated for a moment or two and then very confidently replied, "I can check mail sir."

"Very good, then you will be very useful to me."

Amit replied smiling."Ok then Rajbir, since you know how to E-mail, do this for me... send this mail out to every operator-Airtel, Idea, Vodafone, Reliance," Amit said, giving him a letter.

"Send it from the cyber cell's official ID, you have the password right?"

"Yes sir, I do sir," Rajbir opened up his laptop and set to work.

"Call me as soon as you have received the data," Amit instructed.

"Come on Yadav ji, let's go get a cup of tea meanwhile," Amit called out to the inspector.

"Yes sir, he is a smart chap, he will handle it," Inspector Yadav said, looking towards Rajbir.

"But sir, as I was saying.... why don't we pop over to the site of the crime for a bit, we may find a clue after all," he added.

"No, there's no need for that, I've seen the site on the map," Amit waved away his suggestion.

"But sir, how will you figure out who stole the ATM just by looking into your laptop? At least come and see the state of the ATM. They must have been experts; they have cut through very systematically to steal the machine."

"Yadav Ji... you people have checked out the site properly right? Now, if experienced policemen like you didn't find anything then I sincerely doubt I will find anything else there."

"Yes, yes sir, you are quite right," Yadav slurped on his tea as he replied.

Just then a car, its wheels spinning furiously, pulled up at the police-station. A police officer sporting sunglasses got out from it.

"Dilip sir is here," Inspector Yadav immediately leapt to attention.

"I say, what kind of a production is this... his highness got me pulled out of bed at 7am and is himself just sauntering in, with sunglasses on, no less... Do you think you are in a Bollywood film? Huh?" Amit turned his attention towards Dilip.

"Oh, come on now pal, I have conjunctivitis, if I don't wear the sunglasses I may spread the infection to others," Dilip replied smiling.

"Well, do you think anything can be done here, there is not a damn clue to be found, so I figured you are my best bet?" Dilip continued, placating Amit.

"Yeah, yeah, I am always your best bet. Bet all you like on me, that's probably the only way you will be promoted too; while my life turns to hell in your hands," Amit bantered.

"Sir, I have received the data," Rajbir came running out with the news.

"Great, let's go find these ATM robbers."

Inspector Yadav followed them in, scratching his head and wondering what on earth they would find using just a laptop.

Amit opened his laptop and got busy immediately. Dilip, inspector Yadav and Rajbir stood behind him and peered into his screen over his shoulder.

Thousands of mobile numbers were scrolling up the screen. Amit typed something.

The time-bar on the laptop began to move and after some time two numbers flashed on the screen.

"Here you go, case solved," Amit typed something else and fired out a print-out.

He handed the print-out to Inspector Yadav.

"Here you go... Dalvir Gurjar and Abhinav Tyagi, these are the chaps who stole the ATM."

"Here are their photographs, their mobile numbers... go and arrest them... Abhinav seems to be located in Kavinagar, Ghaziabad... so go and get them."

"What are you saying sir, really? Your laptop gave you all this information?" Yadav still looked disbelieving. He could not understand how a case could possibly be solved this way. And with photographs of the culprits no less!

"But how exactly did you do this sir, please tell us," Rajbir asked eagerly.

"Well, as the ATM was stolen at night between 2 and 4, it obviously could not have been the work of one person alone. It takes time to cut through an ATM cabinet so I assumed at least 2-3 persons were involved. One inside, one outside to keep an eye out for him and warn him and probably one more waiting around the corner in the get away vehicle."

"It is tedious work, to cut through an ATM. Must have taken them a couple of hours at least, tension filled hours. There must definitely have been phone communication between the person inside and the one sitting in the getaway vehicle and keeping an eye out for his partner."

"2 to 4 am is an unusual time for too many people to be in communication. I requested all the operators in this area (Airtel, Idea, Vodafone) to send me their cell tower data, especially for any calls that took place between 2 and 4 am when both parties, that is, the caller and the receiver were present in the same area."

"From the data sent to me, I discovered 2 numbers that had communicated between 2 and 4 am, they had spoken to each other 3 times and both the numbers are from this area only. And the case was thus solved."

"But sir, how did you figure out their names?" Yadav thought for a bit and asked.

"Yadav ji that's the marvel of 'truecaller'!" Amit smiled and replied.

"And the photographs...?"

"Well, if you want I can give you the photographs of their friends and parents too right now."

"What are you saying sir? Really? Just by sitting here?"

"Of course," Amit smiled at him.

"But how sir, do explain."

"It's simple really, 'Truecaller' gave me Abhinav's email ID as well, it's a Gmail ID."

"With this Gmail ID I located his Facebook page and from Facebook I got his photograph."

"Now, if I have his Facebook page, then I have his entire life-history... Come now, where's my reward for all this eh?" Amit turned towards Dilip as he said this.

"Go on then, hand me my reward," Amit said to Dilip.

Dilip smiled and chucked a package towards Amit.

"Got it!" Amit tore through the package jubilantly; his face was lit up with delight.

Inside the package were a broken mobile and some wires...

"Thanks Dilip!" Amit high-fived him and left the police-station.

Inspector Yadav was left wondering... what on earth was it... which had made Amit so happy.

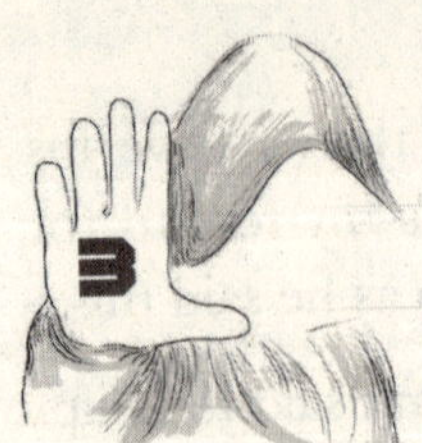

3 THE DEAD CRIMINAL

One who sees inaction in action, and action ininaction, is intelligent among men.

I was just leaving my workplace when I received a call from Kumud."Who is it?" he answered the phone without glancing at the screen.

"Will you be home on time today?" she enquired sarcastically.

"Yes, I was just leaving, I will be home soon," I replied.

"Aparna is here, she is very worried and wants to meet you, we are waiting for you to get home," Kumud said.

"Why, what is wrong?" Aparna is Kumud's friend but it seemed very unusual for her to be at our place at this hour.

"Someone seems to have withdrawn money from her bank account."

"Really! But how?" Although this appeared to be a common enough crime these days, I was surprised as Aparna was not the kind of person to be duped this way, she was smart.

"Just come home, we will tell you in detail, it's not a simple case," saying this, Kumud hung up.

I had just concluded a case regarding a fake call centre and I began thinking about that.

The criminals had been extremely wily and had managed to get away with over 200 Crores.

I wondered if something similar had happened with Aparna.

Kumud answered the door when I got home. Aparna was seated on the sofa in the living room, appearing visibly upset.

"How did this happen?" I got straight to the point upon seeing her obvious distress.

"Around three months ago, I received a friend request on Facebook. It was an old class-mate of mine from school, so I went ahead and accepted the request.

"After a few days, I began to notice that he would 'like' almost all my posts and would also 'comment' on many of my posts.

"Well, that is normal enough, men always tend to like women's posts," I blurted out, realizing my gaffe soon enough when I felt Kumud's eyes glaring at me.

"Yeah, well, go on," I quickly covered up, looking serious.

"I quite liked his comments and the fact that he was 'liking' my posts, so I too began to notice every post he made and started 'Liking' them." Aparna continued with her narration.

"So, did he steal your money?" I was getting impatient now and wanted to get to the point. Once again Kumud's eyes bored into me and I realized that I was rushing her and needed to just sit tight and hear her out.

"What happened after that?" I asked meekly.

"I used to see that he travels a lot internationally- Germany, America, Spain. I thought that he must be in a job in which there must be lot of travel. I used to compliment him for that, and then once he wished me on my birthday over the messenger."

"I also replied back and since then we started chatting on Facebook messenger."

"What kind of chats were they?" I asked curiously.

"Nothing, the chats were usually about his travels."

"What happened afterwards?" I hid my impatience while asking this.

"And then one day I saw his post where he was sitting in a BIG BMW car, somewhere in India probably."

"Wow! Is he extremely rich?" I asked.

"I also thought the same... he was not very good at studies, so how did he earn so much money.. ."

"I asked him excitedly– 'Wow Aniket, how did you earn so much money?' (His name was Aniket)"

"He replied immediately. It is very easy and simple."

"I said– 'Earning money is the most difficult thing'"

"No dear, I don't earn money. Machines earn it for me."

I did not understand anything.

"I am just using an AI based app which earns for me." Aniket said.

"What is that," I was more curious by then. This is a mobile application, which uses artificial intelligence. You know that artificial intelligence, works even better than men. This is a share market app, which invests your money into the share market intelligently and it never makes a wrong decision.

All this sounded new and strange to me. Is this really possible, that a machine earns for you and you get to enjoy the money?

I started studying about artificial intelligence over Google and I realized that Aniket was right.

"Can I also use this app," I asked Aniket the next day "Yes, yes why not- I will just send you the link"– he replied.

As soon as I received the link, I installed the application.

By this time I was totally engrossed in Aparna's story.

"I linked my account with the app and I transferred only Rs 500 into the app at first," she continued.

"When I checked again in the evening, the application showed me that my money had doubled and now I had Rs.1000. I was extremely happy seeing this that a machine was earning for me."

"What happened next?" I asked.

"I used to transfer some money daily and by evening, my money used to double or sometimes even triple. Some days I did not earn much, but yes, this app never gave me any losses."

"I was extremely happy and I had already made plans to buy a big car soon but this morning, when I tried to transfer the money back from the application to my Bank account, I was unable to do it. The application had been blocked."

"After several repeated attempts, when I was still not able to transfer money back to my account, I messaged Aniket but he did not reply back. This was really strange because he used to reply almost immediately."

"I had no other contact of Aniket, so I thought maybe you would be able to help me and I called Kumud."

"Hmmm," I had now understood the whole story.

"Why don't you put a post on your Facebook wall that Aniket has deceived you in such a manner so that other people are aware of his con?"

"I can't put such a post." Aparna said, in a very small voice.

"Varun does not know anything about it."

Varun is Aparna's husband and she did not want him to learn about this incident.

"You just please help me in getting my money back. That's it." She had really high hopes from me.

"Hand me your phone," I told Aparna.

I opened my laptop and connected her mobile to it. After some investigation, it was clear that the app did not work on any artificial intelligence but was a fake app and it just used to create an illusion through the Graphical User interface that your money is increasing but actually your money was just the same as always.

I had understood the truth, and I told Aparna that her money had been transferred to some account in Singapore and from there, it must have been transferred somewhere else.

"What happens now then?" Aparna's face had turned pale.

"Instead of putting effort into getting the money back, we should concentrate on catching the criminal." I replied.

I started doing some internet research on Aniket. I looked at his social media accounts, emails etc. Strangely there was not much information about him over the internet. He just had a Facebook profile, on which I could find some of his photos but when I observed closely, I realized that all of his posts had the same kind of smile and facial expressions, which was very strange.

I thought that I should use OSINT tools to dig deeper about Aniket. OSINT tools are open source software which can search for information about anyone from all nooks and corners of the web.

After some effort, the result was in front of our eyes. I got a piece of information about Aniket from a two and a half year old news-link.

From that news-link, it was clear that Aniket Singh had died in a car accident. The photos of his wife and son were also there in the news-link.

Aniket had died two and a half years back, which means that someone had picked up his old photographs from the internet and morphed them through software, making some new pictures and then he used those pictures to create a Facebook profile, to win the confidence of Aniket's friends and then swindle them.

"Oh my God, this is unbelievable!" Aparna and Kumud were shocked at this revelation.

"Now- what will happen," Aparna was literally in tears.

"Whosoever he is, we will get him in his own game."

"At this time, he does not know that you know everything, so we should try and find his location. I will create a link so that we know his real time location."

"Now you have to send him a message so that he is bound to click on that link."

After some time, Aparna sent him a message.

"Is this true Aniket?" and she sent the "CREATED" link along with the message.

The message had reached him but now we were waiting for him to click the link sent along with the message.

In the meantime, Kumud made coffee for everyone and while we were enjoying our beverage, trying to forget the stress, Aparna started murmuring– 'He must have looted so many people. I wish I had not been greedy.'

She was beginning to lose hope when suddenly I saw an alert on my laptop.

Aniket had clicked the link.

We were able to see the IP address and I started to type furiously on my laptop. I managed to trace his location, which was in Rohini, Delhi.

"This means that it can be someone known to you, a friend probably. Please try to recollect - do you know of anyone who stays in Rohini?" I asked Aparna.

"I don't think so," Aparna said.

I quickly drafted a mail to Facebook legal support and now was awaiting their reply.

"Now please go and get some rest. By morning we will catch this culprit." I told Aparna.

What had I asked Facebook and how would we catch this con man? Aparna was really tense thinking about all this but she trusted me and went home to sleep.

By ten the next morning, we had received the reply from Facebook, and what we came to know was really shocking. Aparna reached our place in another 15 minutes.

"Who is he?" Aparna asked as soon as she entered the house.

I showed her the laptop screen and she was shocked to see Saurabh's photo. How is this possible??

"Yes, he is the culprit and by evening he will be arrested by the Cyber Cell." I informed her.

"Saurabh was also my classmate along with Aniket and Saurabh is also my Facebook friend." Aparna was still in shock.

"Are you sure that it's him?" Aparna reconfirmed.

"Yes- I am 100% sure because the IP address that we got yesterday from Fake Aniket's account was sent to Facebook and we had asked them to tell us whether the same IP address is used to log in to any other Facebook account. I suspected all the time that it had to be someone known, who knew about Aniket's death."

"This morning, Facebook confirmed that Saurabh Shrivastava had also logged in from the same IP address."

Saurabh was caught and he confessed to his crimes.

4 THE SMS WORTH 6.5 LAKHS

Life is what happens when you're busy making other plans

It a place called Auraiya, close to Kanpur Distt. Mr. Ratan Lal had retired from his government job just 2 months ago. After being in service for 35 years in a job where he had often times felt he didn't even have time to breathe, this sudden, endless free time was unnerving.

He had just 2 remaining wishes really. He intended to use his Provident Fund to get his daughter married off in as lavish a way as possible, and with whatever remained he hoped to buy a small piece of farming land and spend the rest of his days tilling soil and communing peacefully with nature.

Mr. Ratan Lal had just stepped out this morning when he received a call on his mobile phone. "Hello, Mr. Ratan Lal? This is Gaurav from OCICI Bank. I wished to speak to you regarding your account with us."

"Yes, please go ahead," Mr. Ratan Lal replied.

"It appears that your Debit card is very old and the Bank has issued new Debit cards to all its customers, so I am calling to let you know that your old card has been blocked."

"But why have you blocked it?" Ratan Lal was perplexed.

"It is to safeguard your money sir. Actually, your old card was magnetic and the newly issued cards are all chip-based."

Mr. Ratan Lal recollected having read in the papers recently that due to the fear of magnetic cards getting cloned very easily these days, banks now, were issuing chip-based cards.

"Alright, but when will I receive my new card? I need to withdraw money, there is a wedding in my family."

"It's very straight forward sir. You go to your bank with your PAN card and your AADHAR card, fill out an application and they will issue you a new card within 4 working days."

"4 days!!? Well, why are you blocking this card now then, can't you do it after I receive my new card?"

"I'm sorry sir, but we have been instructed by the bank to block all magnetic strip cards right away."

"Look, you don't seem to understand, I am extremely busy with some wedding preparations right now and I do not have time to go to the bank to apply for a new card. Let my old card remain active." Ratan Lal sounded angry.

"Please don't get upset sir, hmmm, let me see if I can do something for you," Gaurav tried to pacify him while sounding like he was deep in thought.

"Yes, please do something."

After a few moments, Gaurav's voice came on the line again, "Sir, I may be able to let you continue with your old card for a few more days, however, to do so I will require your permission."

"Yes, yes, you have my permission," Ratan Lal said impatiently.

"No sir, just your verbal permission will not suffice. I am entering your request into our system now, you will receive an SMS shortly, please reply with the numerical 1 to that SMS."

That was easy. Mr. Ratan Lal was pleased that by being stern he had managed to not get his old card blocked after all.

He received an SMS and he immediately replied to it with the number '1'.

"There you go then sir, your old card will now stay active for another month." Gaurav signed off.

Mr. Ratan Lal went straight away to an ATM and withdrew Rs.1000. His old card indeed still appeared to be active.

The next morning, Mr. Ratan Lal was lounging on his sofa when Mr. Shukla dropped by.

"Oh, I tried reaching you on your phone, but could not get through so I thought I would drop by."

"It's your daughter's wedding! You cannot be lolling about!" Mr. Shukla said reproachfully.

"Yes, I know, Mr. Shukla, this Airtel network, it has been giving me a lot of trouble of late," Mr. Ratan Lal smilingly replied.

"Look, I don't have even one bar of the network signal right now," Ratan Lal held out his phone to show Mr. Shukla.

"Well, never mind, let's get out of the house, maybe the signal will be better," said Mr. Shukla.

"Come on, let's go pay a deposit to the Tent man." Mr. Shukla stood up.

"Yes, you're right, let's go. I will withdraw some cash from the ATM on the way too." Mr. Ratan Lal agreed.

At the ATM, Ratan Lal inserted his card and requested for a withdrawal of Rs.10000.

His card popped out of the machine.

"Looks like this machine is out of cash," Ratan Lal smilingly commented.

"Let me have a look, maybe you have entered your PIN wrong."

"Ok, here, you take a look then."

"Oh dear, there appears to be very little balance amount in your account." Mr. Shukla said, sounding distressed.

"Ratan Lal ji, there is only Rs. 700 in your account."

"What are you saying? Maybe you are confusing it with your own account. Just last week my PF has been transferred to my account, I should have 6.5 Lakhs in there!"

"No, really, Ratan Lal ji, have a look for yourself."

"Quick, pull up the mini– statement," Ratan Lal was visibly agitated now.

It was apparent from the mini-statement that Rs. 6.5 lakhs had recently been transferred online from Mr. Ratan Lal's account.

"How is this possible?" Mr. Ratan Lal was pale and his voice shook in disbelief.

"Come on, let's go straightaway to the bank and enquire," Mr. Shukla tried to calm his friend's fear. "Money cannot just disappear this way from a bank account."

But every word out of Mr. Shukla's mouth only made Ratan Lal more and more tense.

"The money from your account has been transferred to a Malaysian account. And it must have been done by you, for it appears that you have used your OTP for it. The bank cannot do anything about it," the clerk at the bank counter drily stated.

"But I have not made this transfer, how can you say this?" Ratan Lal was now very shaken by the clerk's earlier statement.

"You may go and make a complaint at the police station. It may be possible that someone has hacked your phone."

"My phone has been hacked!? What is this man saying?" Ratan Lal turned to his friend, completely worried and perplexed.

I was with Mr. Triveni in the SP Office when Mr. Ratan Lal arrived at the police station.

"Sir, please do something, it was my life long earnings," saying this Ratan Lal burst into uncontrollable sobbing.

Once he had calmed down and was able to talk, I got a handle on his situation fairly quickly.

"Is your phone working?" I asked Ratan Lal.

"Yes, it is on, but I am not able to get a network signal since this morning."

"May I have a look at your phone please?"

I checked his call records and SMS records. In a few seconds it was apparent to me what had occurred.

"You have been made a victim of SIM-swapping," I declared.

"What does that mean?"

"It means that someone has had your SIM issued."

"Mr. Ratan Lal, the person who phoned you pretending to be from OCICI bank, he is the culprit. He was convincing enough to win your trust. He got you to send an SMS from your phone which ended up with your SIM getting blocked. He or they then issued a duplicate SIM from an Airtel counter. This is why you are not getting a signal today; your SIM has been blocked."

"What are you saying? Is this really possible?"

Just one SMS had amounted to Rs. 6.5 lakhs! Mr.Ratan Lal was shocked to come to terms with the fact that that one SMS had cost him 6.5 lakhs, his entire lifetime's savings! He held his head in his hands and burst into sobs.

We tried to pacify Ratan Lal.

The need of the moment however, was to nab these cyber thieves.

We had only 2 clues to lead us to them.

The bank account details to which the money had been fraudulently transferred and the phone number from which Ratan Lal had received the call.

The bank informed us that since the transfer had been made to an International account, it would take some time for them to get any details about the same.

The KYC details about the number from which Ratan Lal received the call also turned out to be fake.

We were now tangled in this and were wondering if any other leads could present us a way out of this situation.

There was definitely something here, something that was not immediately apparent to us.

We went through the entire crime once more, incident by incident.

The criminal phoned Ratan Lal, saying that his debit card has been blocked.

Then he said that he will receive an SMS that he has to reply to.

As soon as Ratan Lal replied to that text message his own SIM card was blocked. The culprit then must have produced a fake I.D at any Airtel centre and got himself a duplicate SIM.

He then installed the BHEEM application on the duplicate SIM and took over complete control of Ratan Lal's bank account.

After that it was easy for him to transfer the entire 6.5 lakhs to a foreign account in Singapore.

"Hmmm...." Mr. Triveni shook his head, puzzled.

"Which server did this spoof SMS originate from, that's the first piece of information we need to digup."

"Also, who issued the duplicate SIM, we need tolocate that Airtel agent ASAP."

The SMS received by Ratan Lal was from a spoof SMS server, but by looking into that server we could obtain an IP address.

We instantly wrote an email to the identified spoof SMS server and asked the details of the user who accessed the server to send an spoof SMS on 7th January, 2019 at 11:16 am to Airtel Server. We asked specifically the IP address of the user.

Triveni Ji instructed Inspector Jitendra to find out the details of the SIM vendor who issues the Ratan Lal Ji's new SIM to the criminal based on some fake Id proof.

"Sir, what will happen now, I have my daughter's marriage in next 20 days. How will I do the arrangements", he started crying with broken heart.

We all knew, what was going through in Ratan Lal Ji's mind.

"Don't you worry, trust us. Not only will we get you your money back, you will be able to hold your daughter's wedding in as lavish a way as you had always hoped to." Mr. Triveni tried to bolster Mr. Ratan Lal.

I glanced at Mr. Triveni as he said these words. The worry on his face, hidden behind his words of encouragement, were plainly visible to me.

"Sir, we couldn't get hold of the vendor who issued the Airtel SIM but we did manage to get some mobile phones and SIM cards from his shop."

"Very good, check the mobile phones, see who all he has communicated with, whether through Facebook, WhatsApp or any other personal apps. We can get a lead on this gang through that mobile phone." Mr. Triveni instructed me.

I began cloning the data on the confiscated mobile phones. Upon analysis of the data I found many AADHAR and PAN card details.

"These people must have fallen prey to a similar stunt I bet," I murmured to myself.

There was a lot of data. Too much information can often times become a hindrance. We did not have much time and it was imperative that we locate the most useful bits of information from this pile.

"Come on, let's take a tea-break," Mr. Triveni suggested, noticing the stress on my face.

Often times we over-complicate certain things to such a degree that the apparent clues are not immediately visible to us.

In an effort to outwit us, criminals try their best to hide themselves but sometimes this very oversmartness result in them making a tiny error.

"Quickly, check, while transferring the money whether the IMEI of the phone used for the transfer is registered?"

"How could I have not thought before to check this?" I held my head in my hands.

In a matter of seconds, we had the IMEI of that mobile phone in front of us.

And whichever SIMs were used on this mobile phone would mostly be cloned SIMs, the criminals had surely pulled the same stunt on other unsuspecting individuals and cloned their SIMs as well.

This idea also did not bear much fruit.

But this time around, we had about 5 IP addresses. We were hoping to zero in on the exact location of the culprits.

Now we needed to get the IP Address log from the BHEEM app server. We needed to compare and see which device's IP address was in use every time that a banking transaction was being made from these accounts.

By that evening we had the server log details. We now had around 17 different IP addresses for when accounts from similar victims were hacked and transactions were made.

When I began to map each IP address to the operators, I was stunned to learn something. "Hey, this is the IP address of Sify Broadband, it belongs to a certain society. Which means during the transactions WiFi was used!"

Now all we needed was to find out from Sify- who was using this particular IP address on this WiFi signal at so and so time.

The next afternoon Inspector Jitendra phoned me, "Sir, we have got the owner address of that IP address. We are on our way there now."

"Alright. Keep me informed and let me know over the phone if you require any help from me," I replied.

The name-board over the door read- Prof. Deepak Chaurasia.

When the police rang the door-bell an old man answered the door.

"Y... yes?" Seeing the police at the door, he seemed a bit shaken.

"We need some information," Inspector Jitendra said.

"Sure, how can I help?"

"Do you use Sify WiFi?"

"Yes... yes, that's right, we do... but what has happened?"

"Who else resides here?" the Inspector glanced around the inside of the house as he asked.

"Only my wife and I," Prof. Chaurasia appeared a bit nervous now.

"On 23rd December, was there anyone else present in your house, someone who could have used your WiFi?"

"No sir, on 23rd December we were not home, we were visiting our son in America. We have just returned, on 5th January,"the professor replied after reflecting for a moment.

Perplexed, the inspector phoned me. "Sir, two elderly people appear to be living here and they claim that on that particular date they were not home. They were in America, visiting their son. I think, maybe Sify has given us the wrong address."

"Hmmm... how many flats are there in that particular building? Ask around; interview the people in nearby flats."

"Especially the flat just above them and the flat below them," I instructed, my mind working furiously now.

"OK, sir," the inspector understood how my mind was working.

After about 20 minutes I received the inspector's call once more, "Sir, I have a feeling we are at the correct location."

"There are 2 young men residing in the flat above. As soon as we entered the flat, it was clear as day. There are numerous fake IDs, SIM cards and mobile phones. I'm quite certain that they have hacked the professor's WiFi on 23rd December."

"We have also got hold of some cash."

"Excellent!" I let out jubilantly and a feeling of satisfaction came over me.

The young men were taken into custody. They admitted that the money recovered from their premises was part of what they had stolen from Ratan Lal and that a part of the money they had transferred to an International account.

I was now relieved and confident with the knowledge that Mr. Ratan Lal would eventually get all his money back and his daughter's wedding would go forth undisturbed.

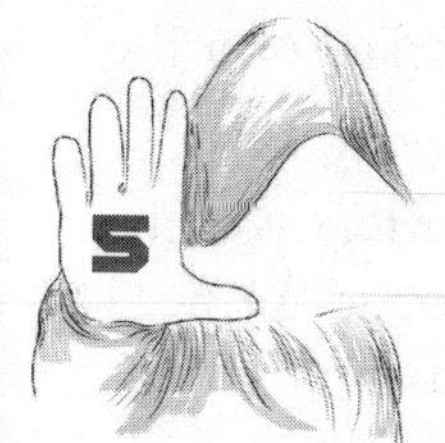

5 THE LAST WISH

A time is envisioned when the world was not, only a watery chaos (the dark, indistinguishable sea) and a warm cosmic breath, which could give an impetus of life

It was late evening and I had just wrapped up a conference in Hyderabad. I was longing to get back to my hotel room and take a nap when my phone buzzed.

"Hi, Amit. Why are you not answering your phone? I have been trying to contact you for so long," Anjana's voice came from the other side.

Anjana is a very famous journalist and news anchor.

"Oh, I had not looked at my phone for a long time.

I was on stage, attending an event." I replied, "What happened?"

"I want your help," She said.

"Yes, please go on."

"I have received an email."

"Who from?"

"I have no idea. It's some girl."

"What is it about?" I asked.

"Her life is in danger, we need to save her."

"Whose life is in danger, who is she?" I asked over the phone.

"We don't have much time. I am forwarding you the mail. Just go through it. You will understand.We need to find the location of this girl as soon as possible," Anjana's voice was trembling.

"We need to find the location of this girl, immediately, as soon as possible," Anjana reiterated.

I had sensed that the issue was something very important and urgent so I quickly responded that I would ring her back after reading the mail.

I opened my mailbox and could see Anjana's mail. I started reading it. The subject of the mail was "The last wish"

> Subject : "The last wish"
>
> Dear Anjana ji,
>
> I am a big fan of yours. The way you speak about some very relevant social issues and are so open minded in your thoughts, it makes me appreciate you even more.
>
> I want that after I die, you may please do a TV show on my story and let the world know that when the society does not support you, when parents, brother, sisters, no one supports you, then suicide seems to be the only solution.
>
> I am tired and have lost this battle. Maybe some other person could benefit from my story and we can save someone's life through my story.
>
> My life is passing through a strange phase, and I have decided that I will end my life today.

I have no idea when you will read my story or maybe you don't even read it, still with a glimmer of hope I am telling you my story.

This is a long story and I don't know where I should begin.

Three years back, I had started working as a pharmacist with a hospital. One year prior to starting the job, I had contracted tuberculosis. My case was very peculiar and complicated but still I survived. When I had joined the hospital I was not fully cured and I was still under medication. I was quite bored with life and around this time I met a man in the hospital and we became good friends. We started going on dates and started spending time together. After some time, both of us realized that we had fallen in love but both of us were extremely terrified because we belonged to two different religions. I am a Hindu and he is a Muslim. Despite knowing this fact, we both had decided to be together forever and we started living like husband and wife, we started putting together our savings and we even made certain investments together.

I always knew that my family will never approve of this relationship. And the expected happened when my brother came to know of our relationship. Though my brother is a doctor he is still very conservative. He called up my boyfriend's father and warned him of very severe consequences. Then he also beat me black and blue, and a hard slap from him damaged my eardrum due to which I lost the hearing capability from one ear.

Now the situation was such that we couldn't see each other, which is why one of us had to leave the job. He decided to quit so that I could continue working and be independent. Our families thought that we had ended our relationship, but we now had a stronger resolve to keep our relationship alive and we were much more serious this time. We always used to think as to how we can make our families understand our love for each other. Though we had now decided that even if they don't agree, we would still be together and I will leave my family. Atik had decided to start a new business and had even started working on it. I realized that my brother was tracking all my moves, due to which I was so scared that I decided not to talk to Atik when I was at home. My brother was hounding me like a detective and I was scared that if he senses anything fishy, he will beat me again. I used to talk to Atik only when I was in office and I used to delete all the records of that call, so that my brother would not come to know of it. And due to all this pressure and restrictions, I used to shout at Atik often, but he is such a nice guy, he understood me completely and never complained.

10 Feb, 2015 was a day that changed my life completely. I was getting ready for office when my mother and my sister came to me with a man's photo and wanted me to see it so that I

can marry him. I immediately refused which made them think that I am still in touch with Atik and they decided to lock me in a room. I somehow managed to escape from there and I immediately called up Atik. Atik told his parents but they were of the view that we should get married only if my parents also agree and give their approval. I knew that they would never agree to my marriage with Atik because of his religion.

Atik's father was right in a way because my brother had warned him of dire consequences if Atik and I formed any relationship and Atik was their only son. I was adamant that we should certainly get married, but Atik did not want to marry me against his father's wish. We thought a lot but finally we decided to break up our relationship.

Since then I am totally heart broken. I have also started keeping unwell. Earlier my weight used to be around 50kgs but I have reduced to 40 kgs now. I tried earlier also once to take my life by eating sleeping pills but I somehow survived. I had thought that my suicide attempts might calm my parents down and they might agree for me to marry Atik but they are still the same and arc adamant on their stand against Atik.

I don't talk to anyone in my family now and it seems they also do not care about me at all. They say that if I marry into a Muslim family, they will force me to eat meat and they will forcefully ask me to wear a burqa and what not.

My last wish is that you should show my story on your news channel. I have already lost my love and I can't marry him. I am highly depressed. I have even talked to a psychologist but they only give medicines but no medicine can give me back the love of my life. I can only be cured if I get my love back. I even talked to my friends and they all suggest that I should move on with my life. It's been 8 months since Atik and I broke up, but I have not been able to move on with my life. I don't see any reason to be alive now. My life has become colourless, so I will end my life. Please show my story to this big bad world. I have no options left now. I don't think anyone is going to be affected by my death so it's better to die. Good bye Ma'am.

Your fan,

Ritu Chhabra

Apart from this mail, we did not have any clue about the where abouts of this girl. We just had one mail and this girl could commit suicide at anytime. Our job was not only to find her but also stop her from committing suicide. In a country with a population of 125 crores, this girl could be in any corner, a village or a city....

I called up Anjana. "Do you know this girl by any chance? Have you received any phone call from her, where she might have tried to say something but you might have been busy, so you might have cut the call? Please try to remember anything that you can. Any WhatsApp or SMS?" I said.

"No, I don't recall any such thing," Anjana replied.

"I don't think this girl has my number. She just picked up my email from my website and emailed me," Anjana said thoughtfully.

"Amit, please find this girl. I can't let her die, otherwise I will never be able to forgive myself."Anjana got very emotional.

"Don't worry. I will try my best." I assured her.

Now the onus was on me and I was tense because I did not know from where to begin my search for her.

I started off by trying to find her IP address. Usually we can find the IP address through the email header but unfortunately I could not find the IP address from the email address.

I decided to reply to her email thinking that I will try to convince her to live and give her some motivation. I was hopeful that she might change her decision.

> Dear Ritu,
>
> We don't know each other but I being more experienced than you, I can assure you that life is a beautiful journey. God has sent us all with some purpose. I can understand your emotions completely because I myself have gone through similar troubles. I also wanted to do the same thing as what you are thinking, but now after so many years, I think what a fool I was.
>
> In this world, there are so many beautiful experiences, so many beautiful things, that you can't even imagine. I and Anjana are really worried for you. We want to talk to you. Please call me on 65436262.
>
> With many best wishes,
>
> Amit

While sending the mail, I also added an IP logger to the mail, so that whenever she opens up her mail, I should come to know of her IP address and through her IP address, I will try to reach her location. But we could not sit and relax assuming that she will open her email. What if she tries to commit suicide before opening the email? So, I tried finding clues through her email sent to Anajna. I read it several times and could conclude the following points:

Girl's name is Ritu Chhabra.

She is a pharmacist.

The girl's age should be almost 25-26 years because she has been working for 3 years after finishing college.

Her boyfriend is a Muslim and his name is Atik.

Her brother is a doctor.

She is appointed in some hospital, so I assume she must be in some city.

With all this information, I started searching for Ritu Chhabra over Facebook. That Ritu Chhabra who is a pharmacist, who is 25-26 years old. I could find some 8 profiles and in those 8 profiles, I started looking for a girl who has tagged a Muslim friend named Atik, who also is a pharmacist and it didn't take me long to reach the profile of this Ritu Chhabra.

So according to this profile, Ritu was a resident of Mumbai. But I needed more information so that we could pin-point her location. I thoroughly scanned her profile to see if she has tagged her location anytime, maybe of a restaurant or of her work location but unfortunately I could not find any tagged locations. Moreover her last post was 2 months old, so her last logged in location might also not be of any use. Strangely, none of Ritu's family members were a part of her friends list. No "Chhabra" profile was a friend but I had her boyfriend's Atik Ansari's profile. So I started scanning Atik's profile. But even Atik's profile had not been active since the past 3 months. He had very few friends so I left that profile and started scanning Ritu's profile again. I was trying to find some of Ritu's friends who stayed in Mumbai and had their email address updated on Facebook. I mailed a few of Ritu's friends with the Subject – "Please help in finding Ritu Chhabra."

It was midnight; I was extremely exhausted and was unable to think anything. I knew that my staying awake was very important so I made myself some tea and sat on the sofa staring at the wall clock in front of me. Every passing moment was making me feel dizzier.

I had just started sipping my tea when an alert came on my phone. It was an IP logger alert, which meant that Ritu had opened the mail. I checked the IP address and it was showing some location in Powai which meant that she could be anywhere in the vicinity of that location up to 8-10 kms. She had opened the mail which meant she was still alive and according to my script, she had opened her mail on an Android phone, her internet operator was Airtel, but I still could not retrieve her mobile number. She had replied to me.

> Dear Sir,
>
> Thanks for your kind words. Please convey my thanks to Anjana ji as well but talking to you or Anjana ji won't change my decision. I have already lost my love forever. I don't even

trust God now. My family thinks that I have stopped following any rituals because I am now following Muslim culture. My father even hit me once when I said that I don't want to be a part of the Diwali Aarti.

Also Sir, I am no longer a small kid. I am a 25 year old professional and still no one considers me anything. Anyone can hit me anytime. I can't tolerate this anymore. I want to thank you and Anjana Ma'am once again for showing your sympathy towards me but I have decided to end my life. I am just finishing off a few tasks. Please ask Anjana ma'am to definitely make the show on my story.

Regards,
Ritu

At around 00:05 midnight, I called up Triveni Ji.

"Sir, we have got the IP address, we even know the operator. Kindly ask the cyber cell to let us know that at 00:03, whose phone was given this IP address. If we can know the mobile number, then we will be able to get the exact location of the girl and we might reach in time to save her.

"What is the location?" Triveni Ji asked.

"Powai, Mumbai."

"Ok, I will give you the number of the inspector posted at Powai Police Station. Talk to him and send him Ritu's photo. He will check in the neighbouring societies, if anyone happens to know this girl. And send me the IP and timestamp; I will try to find out her mobile number."

"Ok, Sir", I sent him the IP and timestamp.

I was a little confident now because in her mail, Ritu had mentioned that she had to finish off certain tasks before committing suicide, which will give us a little more time to save her. Probably.

I thought of writing another mail to her.

> Dear Ritu,
>
> We want to talk to you because we are really very worried about you. As I told you earlier, I have also had some similar experiences in my life and I can totally understand your emotions. When we pass through such phases in life, then life seems to be so meaningless.
>
> But life is absolutely beautiful. I am sure you will also realize this sooner or later. Love, hate, jealousy, anger, these emotions keep coming and going but you have a bigger purpose in life, much bigger than these small emotions. You should talk to us. Don't be scared to talk. We want to talk to you just like a friend. May be we can help you because we are much more experienced than you. Even after talking to us, if you feel your decision is correct, then you may go ahead with your decision. What is the harm in talking to us at least once?
>
> Life has in store some beautiful surprises for you, don't give up so easily. You are an intelligent girl and I understand that you have achieved success in your life through lots of hard work. I am really impressed by the purity of your thoughts and I want that

the world should learn from your experience and get inspired by you.

Just give yourself 3-4 months and I assure you that all these people will listen to you and will work towards fulfilling your wishes. Please talk to us once and we will certainly find a solution to your problems.

Hoping to speak to you soon.

Amit Dubey

Now again I was waiting. Will she read the mail? Will the mail make an impact?

All these thoughts were crossing my mind and I don't know when I fell asleep.

In the morning, I woke up to the ringing of my phone. I opened my eyes with great difficulty and answered the phone. The call was from an unknown number.

"Hello Sir, this is Akash speaking. I got your mail regarding Ritu", the unknown voice said.

"Yes, yes, do you know Ritu? Do you know where she stays?" I asked Akash.

"But why do you want to meet her Sir?" Akash asked.

"Ritu is very disturbed and is about to commit suicide and we want to save her," I said impatiently.

"Oh– sorry sir. Please note down her address and her phone number," Akash gave the important information that we had been looking for.

The email ID of Ritu's friend which we got through Facebook analysis had done the trick for us.

The rest of the job now seemed easier. I immediately called up the Powai area Inspector and asked him to find Ritu by giving him the address and phone number. I also gave him clear instructions that we don't have to scare her, rather we have to make her understand.

I had just sat down to breakfast when the inspector called and told me that he had found Ritu. He gave the phone to Ritu.

"Hello Ritu, this is Amit Dubey", I said.

"I am surprised sir, that I had just mailed you and you tracked me down in even less than 10 hours", Ritu sounded a little happy this time.

"This is my job Ritu," I said.

"But for me this is a miracle Sir," Ritu replied.

"It will be a miracle only if we are able to make you understand the importance of life," I tried to convince her.

"Sir, my life is not that simple," Ritu said.

"I know that Ritu," I tried to assure her.

"No Sir, you only know half the truth," Ritu replied.

"What do you mean?" I enquired.

"Someone is blackmailing me." Ritu said.

"Who?" I asked.

"I am not sure sir, but he has some of my pictures which I can't let anyone know about," Ritu said in a lower voice this time.

"Do you know of anyone who can do this? And how did these pictures reach him?" I was surprised.

"I don't know sir. I can't share this with anyone, not even with my boyfriend, so I am left all alone and depressed, fighting with all this. Now, after talking to you, I am feeling somewhat hopeful, that if you can find me, just by an email, then you can find this blackmailer too." Ritu sounded a little hopeful now.

So now the onus was back on me to fit in all the pieces of the story.

"Don't worry, we will catch hold of this blackmailer. I am coming to Mumbai to meet you," I assured her.

After two days, I reached Mumbai. Ritu was waiting for me in the investigation room with one of her friends.

She introduced me to her friend, Aarti.

"So, you have not told this to anyone in your family?" I asked.

"No Sir, I cannot tell them. They will beat me even more", she replied.

"Face the truth Ritu, There must be someone with whom you can share your story", I said.

"Sir, you please find the blackmailer and then I will tell my family", she replied.

"Deal", I smiled back.

"So, let me know minutest details that you can recollect. Just think if someone else also likes you, someone whom you might have had a fight with, any shop owner where you get your mobile recharged? Any person or any place that you suspect? Give me all details."

We talked for about an hour but somehow it didn't lead to anyone whom we could suspect. So we went back to doing the Facebook analysis of Ritu's page. After a few minutes, I could see one thing which seemed to be abnormal. I could see one post of Ritu about 6 months old where she had mentioned that she has lost her mobile phone and had asked her friends to share their contact details again. Ritu had shared this post from her laptop.

As such this post was not abnormal but the next post made it all clear to me. In the next post Ritu had mentioned– "Thank God, I got my mobile phone back". Now, this post was shared from her "lost and found" mobile phone.

Normally, I have never seen people getting back their lost mobile phones.

So I asked Ritu– "How did you get your mobile phone back?"

"The security guard of the office gave it to me", Ritu replied.

When I asked the security guard how he got the phone, he replied that he got it from a child who works in a nearby restaurant.

We could not find that child, but I was now sure that the phone was stolen with a purpose and that is why it was returned back.

"I will have to scan your phone", I took Ritu's mobile and connected it to the laptop, for scanning.

In a few minutes, the truth was in front of us. There was a Trojan virus in her phone.

Ritu was inquisitive and she asked– "What is Trojan virus?"

"Someone is controlling your phone remotely. They can switch on the camera, capture photos, view every message, view every photo, video, everything."

Ritu was shocked.

Both of us now wanted to know the person who is doing this. I checked where all this data is going. When I analyzed the Trojan further, it revealed that this application is sending all this data on a server, whose IP address is of a location in Israel.

But this information was not enough to get to the criminal. We were so close yet so far from the criminal. He could be anybody but this was for sure, that criminal was not somebody from out of the country, He was around us as he knew Ritu very well.

But who was he? I was trying hard to find him.

It was important to connect the end of these stories so I re-analyzed Ritu's Facebook account, but this time through a new analysis tool which took about 4 hours to give me the result.

The analysis tool revealed that in Ritu's friend list, there were two closed groups which made a loop with Ritu.

In both of these groups, Ritu was friend of only two people but there were 5 more people, those were connected to these two people and had a loop connection.

Atik was a common friend in both of these groups but there were 3 girls too.

I also noticed that the people in these groups, other than Ritu, were really very active for almost a period of one year and usually liked and commented almost every post of Atik. But since the last 4 months, their activities were nil. This was strange.

In fact since last 5 months, Atik's and Ritu's accounts were also not very active. There was something between these groups and Ritu which I was unable to understand.

So I started looking into each and every profile of these groups, I analyzed them at depth and what I found was truly unbelievable.

One by one, the truths got revealed and we found that all the accounts of these groups were fake. Almost eleven Facebook accounts.

Only two people were real in these groups, Ritu and Atik. All the other Facebook profiles were fake.

There was someone, who had created eleven Facebook accounts and wanted the proximity with Ritu and Atik.

Now we wanted to find out from where, exactly, were these Facebook accounts being operated? We made a request to Facebook legal through 91 CRPC and received their response which finally revealed everything.

We received all the IP addresses from where these accounts were operated.

(IP address is the unique identification to your mobile and laptop which is assigned to you by internet service provider when you access the internet).

All these accounts were operated from same IP address.

Which meant there was this single person who was managing all these fake Facebook profiles.

We then mapped these IP addresses to the device IDs and we found his mobile number through the IMEI number.

The moment we received the mobile number, I asked the inspector to bring this person to the police station.

The case was solved, we just wanted a statement from Ritu.

We called Ritu as well and I explained everything to her. I asked her whether she had ever met any of these eleven people.

She shook her head.

I asked her whether she would like to meet them.

She looked at me, puzzled. “Come follow me,” I gestured and she started walking behind me.

In a few minutes, we were in front of a door.

Come Ritu, let me introduce you to the person who is behind these eleven Facebook profiles.

I opened the door and Ritu got the shock of her life when she noticed the person sitting in that room.

She was frozen for a moment.

“A- Atik you?” she could only say this.

She was shivering with anger. She collapsed to the floor, put her head to her knees and started crying.

Friends, why did Atik do all this and how did a magical world created on social media come crashing down in a moment?

The characters of this story does not allow us to share those details.

6 THE CRIMINAL MOBILE GAME

When I accept myself, I am freed from the burden of needing you to accept me

It was late evening and I had just wrapped up a conference in Hyderabad. I was longing to get This is an incident that occurred sometime in December 2010. I was working on NOKIA phones those days and I was in Finland at the time. We were working on the NOKIA N-95 series when I received a message from the Paris Police. They needed my help to investigate a certain mobile phone, so I left for Paris.

When I arrived at Paris, I learned that this case belonged to a town that was a few hours away from Paris.

Mrs. Maria had received an anonymous phone call from a person. The caller said that Mrs. Maria's daughter had been kidnapped and unless she transferred 25,000 pounds, within an hour, to a certain account the consequences would be dire.

At first, Maria took this to be a prank call and disconnected the phone.

10 minutes later she received another call. "Don't make the mistake of taking my words lightly; you will end up

repenting your whole life. You now have just 50 minutes left. Transfer the money or else..."

Maria was scared now. This happened in those days when mobiles were not as common, not everyone had one. Her daughter was out and Maria had no way of contacting her.

The situation appeared grim. She tried to negotiate with the caller. "I don't have this much money in my account. I cannot make the transfer so quickly. Please, I think you must be mistaken. I am not a rich person."

"Don't take me for a fool, I know exactly how rich you are," the caller barked back angrily.

"Please, please believe me, I do not have this much money in my account," Maria was close to tears.

What the caller said next shook Maria to the core.

"Mrs. Maria, the bedroom in which you are right now has a painting on the far wall which itself is worth at least 5000 pounds. Don't try to educate me on how rich you are or are not. Transfer the money immediately."

Maria froze for a moment; she glanced over her shoulder at the painting hanging on the wall behind her and then ran out into the drawing room.

"No, no, you are mistaken, there is no such painting here," Maria tried to sound calm.

"I am not mistaken Madame, there is a vase in the corner of the drawing room where you are now, that vase too is worth about 2000 pounds. May I remind you, you only have 40 minutes left now...," the caller threatened

Maria was now convinced that the caller was watching her somehow. She had no choice left but to do as he said. She quickly opened her laptop and transferred 25000 pounds.

40 minutes later her daughter walked into the house, safe and sound.

Nobody had kidnapped her.

Maria was mystified. She was at a complete loss trying to figure out what had actually happened. She went to the police. The police did a thorough search of her house but they could not locate any hidden cameras or any other kind of surveillance devices.

The police were confounded as well. How did a fake kidnapper manage to convince Maria that he was watching her live?

All their investigations finally ended with them finally focussing on Maria's mobile phone.

The police were quite certain that this was definitely something to do with the mobile phone through which the anonymous caller had created the illusion that he could see Maria live.

Maria's phone was a NOKIA N95 and thus I was summoned to investigate it.

I scanned the phone thoroughly but I could not find any wires or anything else in the least suspicious about it.

I was myself very concerned and restless and was trying my best to unearth any sort of clue. I stepped out to get myself a coffee, at the coffee shop I noticed a young man playing a game on his mobile phone.

I thought I too would play a game to distract myself for a bit. I looked through Maria's phone to see whether there were any games there. I found one.

The game was called Truefighter.

This game was sort of similar to Pokemon Go. The camera on the phone worked as a view- finder and if you walked along the wall with your phone, virtual objects like spiders would appear through the camera.

On clicking pictures of these virtual objects you gained points.

Oh my goodness! This was a 'eureka' moment for me. I asked Maria immediately who played this game in her house.

I think my son plays it. He's 9.

I began analysing this game. I learned that through this game around 150 photos of Maria's home had been sent; which meant that someone had photos of almost every room and wall of Maria's house.

One thing was for sure, this game had been installed onto this phone for a purpose.

Upon investigating further, I learned that the IP address of the server to which these photos had been sent was located somewhere in Turkey; which wasn't of much use to me.

The bigger mystery for me was to figure out how the caller knew which room Maria was in at any given time whilst speaking to her.

GPS is used to approximately locate a phone. But this usually works out of doors; using GPS to locate a phone while indoors is just not possible.

This case had turned into a personal challenge for me now. I just had to figure out what kind of technology this was; technology that was enabling the caller to know exactly which room in her house Maria was standing in when she was speaking to him.

I had been in Europe for almost 45 days now; Christmas was approaching, there was festivity in the air and all around.

I strolled through the streets, taking pictures and then I walked back to my hotel.

I glanced at my phone to check the time; it was 5:00 pm which meant it would be 9:30 pm in India; so I made a Skype call to Kumud.

I kept feeling that I was very close to cracking this case... it was just a tiny but obvious clue that was eluding me.

"What is it that you can't find?" Kumud asked me, raising her voice to be heard.

"A clue... I can't find a clue!" I answered back, raising my voice too.

"Hang on, I can't hear you clearly, let me move to the room with the WiFi router, will get a better signal then," Kumud hollered.

"What did you say... room with the WiFi... OH MY GOD!" everything fell into place suddenly.

"Kumud, thank you! I will ring you back; I think I have found my clue!" I was jubilant.

"What clue... what did I say..." Kumud was very puzzled. But I knew now... and I knew what I had to do next.

I began clicking photos once again through the game. This time when I analysed the upload packets I noticed that with every photo the WiFi signal strength was also being sent. The WiFi signal strength was helping the criminal map every room of that house; when he called he could thus tell, just by the strength of the WiFi signal at the time the exact location of the person inside the house.

Wow! This was amazing! I was just discovering that WiFi could be used to track a person's indoor location as well!

This criminal is an advanced level programmer, I thought to myself.

Back in 2011 this technology was almost unheard of, therefore I could assume that this person was either a scientist or was friends with a scientist.

I began to search on Google- 'Indoor positioning using WiFi signals'.

Within an hour or two of tedious searching effort, I had in front of me, a list of all persons who were into this research.

With the help of the police I began to get in touch with these people to enquire whether any of them had developed or gotten developed the Symbian mobile app, for any kind of demo.

Meanwhile I also emailed Symbian support asking them if they could let me know the details of the person whose ID was used to sign for this app.

Just like today's Android Operating System, those days Nokia was using the Symbian Operating System. However, if you created any applications on Symbian, the Symbian management required you to digitally sign for it. In this way the Symbian management could control that any app created had been created by an authorized developer alone.

I began comparing the list of professors and scientists that I had found on Google against the list of developer profiles that I received from Symbian App developer. I soon learned that the developer who had created this game app was a research student from the University of Oulu. I also found his professor's research paper which was about 'WiFi based location tracking'. We were close to cracking this case now.

Police investigation confirmed that this app had been developed in this University. The professor also admitted to it but he was astounded to learn how a crime could have been committed using this particular app.

The actual culprit was still eluding us.

On the insistence of the police, the professor shared with us a list of all the students involved in the project. We had with us a list of 17 students; their names and details. Again, with the help of the police there began an enquiry into each of those 17 students; their bank accounts were checked; their bank accounts, life-styles and spending patterns were looked into. Each and every one of those students was also made to speak on the phone with Mrs. Maria in the hope that she may recognize one of their voices.

But nothing came of all this.

Often times having come this close to solving a case but still not succeeding was a terribly dreadful feeling. I was at the airport; while sitting there I noticed a child playing a game on a mobile phone.

An idea struck me all of a sudden.

How could I have missed this?

I phoned the Investigation Officer straightaway. "Sir, I need these details please, as soon as possible!"

Brilliant! That was the IO's response. He requested me to stay on at Oulu for a few more days, he was certain now that we would apprehend the criminal.

The Symbian server logged the details of all the mobiles that had this particular app installed. Whoever had used this app for this criminal purpose must definitely have tested it beforehand. We had to find out from Symbian, the details of the mobiles where this app was first installed. The culprit had to amongst that list.

In a short while, we had a list of 50 mobiles that were among the first to install this app. It was then easy to find out which among these 50 were located in the Oulu region.

When the police raided that particular student, they found photos of Mrs. Maria's house on his laptop.

7 FACEBOOK LIKE AND 3700 CRORE

It is not the man who has too little,
but the man who craves more, that is poor

It was late evening and I had just wrapped up a conference in Hyderabad. I was longing to get I was sitting in North Avenue with Satyendra ji, who is an Income tax commissioner. Satyendra ji was giving his opinion on the social media revolution in the country– "These days, social media has a big influence on people, everyone is busy making their image better on the media. The number of likes on Facebook and Instagram decide how popular you are."

"You are right Sir. Even politicians are struggling on a day-to-day basis to increase their fan following on Twitter and Facebook," I said supporting his statement.

"Just recently, my driver was telling me that he works for a digital marketing company where he is sent a Facebook link and he just has to like it and he is paid for it," Satyendra ji continued.

"You are right sir, this is all becoming a business, there are quite a few digital marketing companies who take money from you and through bogus accounts and votes, they increase the number of followers of people on Twitter and Facebook."

"Yeah, but he is making a lot of money out of it. Yesterday only he got a cheque of 15000 rupees", Satyendra ji said with both shock as well as enthusiasm. "He might stop working for me one day if he keeps earning this much," he laughed.

"15000 Rupees?" I was shocked.

"Yes yes, he was telling me that for every page that he likes, he gets 5 rupees for that. His wife does the same job the whole day and she earns 1000-1200 rupees in a day!"

"Sir, I really sense something fishy here. Who will pay Rs 5 per like?"

"Don't bother, I will prove it right away, let me call Pramod, my driver, here and you can ask him yourself".

"Please ask Pramod to come to me," he ordered his peon and in few minutes Pramod was standing in front of both of us.

"What was the amount of the cheque that you received yesterday? Just show it to Sir."

"Sir– Full fifteen thousand rupees," he said with great pride and took out the cheque and showed it to me.

I studied the cheque in and out. The cheque was issued by a company named Blade Info Systems.

"Please deposit it quickly," I told the driver.

While I was returning from Satyendra ji's office, my mind was continuously thinking about the same thing. Is it really true that a company can pay you so much just for liking a Facebook page?

After reaching home, I checked social media marketing companies offers over the web just tosee what was the ongoing rate for these kind of likes but nowhere could I find a rate exceeding twenty or twenty five paise.

I was still shocked as to how a company could offer 5 rupees per like.

Next day, when I woke up, I heard the conversation between our house help, Lakshmi and Kumud.

"Ma'am, please trust me, I will return your money within a few days," Lakshmi was saying.

"How will you return so much money in just four weeks?" Kumud asked surprised.

"Ma'am, my paternal uncle's son and his wife earned 5000 rupees in just one week, so I will earn twenty thousand this month," Lakshmi said confidently.

"These are all frauds, don't get yourself into all this, I am warning you," Kumud told Lakshmi.

"She is asking for twenty thousand rupees as an advance. She is saying she will return it in one month," Kumud tried to explain me the gist of the conversation.

"But why do you need twenty thousand rupees?" I asked while rubbing my eye.

"I just have to deposit the subscription fees, I already have Rs. 30000 and I need another twenty thousand to pay the fees," Lakshmi replied.

"What subscription fees?" I asked Lakshmi, while looking at Kumud.

Kumud then explained that Lakshmi was talking about some company which pays you for liking the links that they send and for every like on Facebook, they pay Rs.5 and to subscribe for this service, you need to pay one time registration amount and based on your registration amount, they send 25, 50 or 100 links on a daily basis.

Ok, this scheme has even reached my house. I thought to myself.

"What is the name of the company who is offering this?"– I asked Lakshmi.

"Something Blade Bhaiya,"– Lakshmi replied.

"Just wait for one or two days, I am sensing something wrong here. Let me investigate and then I will give you the subscription money."

"Bhaiya, they will increase the subscription fees by then. Please understand. This offer is only for today and for select people. If you don't give me money, I will keep my bangles for mortgage and pick money from the market," Lakshmi said.

"No, don't ever do this foolishness", Kumud warned her.

Each and every word of Lakshmi's was proof that something really fishy was going on but at this point in time, making Lakshmi understand was really difficult, so I immediately called up Prof. Triveni Singh.

"Sir, I want to meet you."

"Yes, please come over, I am in office only", He said And in a few minutes I reached his office.

But before I could say anything, he showed me a photo of a 20-22 year old youth.

"What has he done?", I asked inquisitively.

"He has fooled at least 12000 people"

"How?"

He typed on the browser.

http://rrbbpl.nic.in/

"What is this?"

"It's a railway recruitment website", He said.

"And now see this", He typed again on the browser window- www.rrbbpl.org

"And this is also a railway recruitment board site", I was looking at it.

"Yes but this is a fraud website", he looked at me.

"What? This looks even better than the original one", I was surprised.

"This boy was running this site and posted railways jobs on this website. Then he collected lots of application fees from innocent individuals looking for job. To make his fake website look real, he even linked his fake website to the original website."

"And a similar such story is being repeated here in Noida also. Someone is running a fake scheme to fool the innocents, where money is promised for as many facebook likes, but for that you need to pay the registration fees", I said.

"And who is running this fake scheme?"

"Sir, there is some company by the name Blade Info Systems, here in Noida only."

"Ok, Let me check", Triveni ji asked about the same on his police only whatsapp group and he got a reply in some time.

"Yes– there is a case registered in Phase– 2 police chowki where the victim has complained of not receiving the money but this needs more investigation and some evidence."

"The people who have already taken a subscription and are being sent these links, I would like to call them and start my investigation", I said.

In some time, I had in front of me 12 people who were receiving 25 or 50 links daily.

After seeing those links, it was apparent that these Facebook pages had nothing, for which someone will pay to promote it and get more likes.

And then we analysed the time of creation and creation location of those pages and the picture was clear now.

Mostly the pages were new and they were created almost all at the same time.

And the most surprising thing was that all these pages were created from the same network, which meant that the same company had created those pages. Information about 150-200 pages such pages was in front of us.

Why did the company create so many pages and why are they promoting these pages and giving 5 rupees for every like, and how much money are they earning out of it, these questions were still to be answered.

Our apprehensions were turning out to be true.

"Without raiding the company, can we get the information about how big this scam can be and how many people have been victimized?"– Triveni ji asked me.

"Yes– just by looking at these pages, we can analyse that also."

"See sir", I turned my laptop towards him.

"All of these pages have some 10-12 lakh likes, it's obvious that these likes have been done by the innocent people who were sent these links"

After a little more analysis it was clear that some 6-7 lakh likes had been done by real Facebook profiles.

"6-7 Lakhs? If every person has paid about 50000 rupees, then the company has some 3500 crore Rupees", Triveni ji was shocked.

"Quite possible sir and the people who have liked these pages, we can get the details about them from the analysis of these pages only", I suggested.

"Please check the locations of the people who have liked these pages. From there we will know where is this group active." Triveni ji suggested and after the analysis, a map came up.

We were exasperated to see that they are active in almost all regions but mostly in north and mid India.

"After analysis of the bank accounts and finances of the company, we will be sure if there is any other source of income of the company apart from the registration fees", Triveni ji was thinking.

"I don't think they have any business model, they are thriving on this fraud scheme and must be investing this money somewhere outside India."

"We have quite a few details now and now its time for action", Triveni ji said.

The team of STF raided Blade Info Systems the next day and arrested the owner Mr. Sunil Goyal. His wife and father were also arrested along with him.

While investigating the case, because it was related to money laundering, so the enforcement directorate was also involved.

Next day the news headlines made a furore all over India that a company which dealt with facebook likes had made a whopping 3700 crores and it had victimied almost 8 lakh people. The truth was even more shocking that the master-mind behind this crime was a 25-year-old engineering student from Noida.

"25 years and 3600 crores– Wow", I had just picked up the paper when Lakshmi entered.

"Bhaiya– that company was a fraud and they looted lakhs of people", She said.

"Yes– its there all over the news", I showed her the paper.

"Will they ever be returned their money Bhaiya. Some people had even mortgaged their houses to invest in the scheme."She asked I had no answer to Lakshmi's question.

8 AN ONLINE COMPLAINT AND ROBBERY

Don't be a slave to the desire of your virtual world

Deepak Bhasin was head of an IT company.

"Oh dear, there is again something wrong with the water purifier. Will you come and take a look at it please," Jyoti called out. Jyoti is Deepak's wife and an IT consultant as well.

"Oh... yes... I somehow missed the helpline number of this RO Company, which is why I could not put in a complaint yesterday," Deepak replied.

"C'mon Deepak, just Google it, you fill find their helpline number as well as their helpline page," Jyoti suggested.

Deepak Googled and found the Livpure Water Purifiers Helpline number.

"Oh yes, here it is," Deepak had also found the earlier link which contained a helpline page.

Deepak made a complaint and filled out the additional details required by them.

"The service person will come at 2 pm today, I have given them your number, you come in early from office please," Deepak said to Jyoti.

"Yeah sure, thanks, I will make sure I am there at home."

Deepak was at work in his office at 2 pm when he received a call from Jyoti.

"The RO serviceman is here, he's asking for Rs.8000 to replace the filter and the cylinder," Jyoti informed him.

"Put him on, I'll have a word with him," Deepak said.

"Yes sir, this is Patvardhan speaking, of Livpure servicing. When did you last get your filter serviced?"

"We have been getting it serviced quite regularly but we have been travelling a lot so probably haven't got it serviced in the last 3-4 months."

"Mr. Bhasin, the cylinder and filter both require replacement; it's going to cost you Rs. 8000."

"Goodness, 8000 is a lot my friend, for that kind of money I could buy a new RO filter."

"Sir, I'm just telling you the price of the parts needed to be replaced as your product is no longer under warranty; I'm not even going to charge you for my services."

"Even so... 8000 is a bit much; give me a decent rate otherwise I might as well get a new RO filter."

"But sir, you will have to pay the cost of the parts; if you want I could suggest a nice scheme which will help you."

"What scheme?"

"If you like, I can give you a back-dated warranty of 3 years; that way the replacement of parts will cost you nothing and for the next 2 years as well you can get parts replaced for free."

"Is that really possible," Deepak asked, astounded.

"Anything is possible sir, I can do it for you, 3 years warranty including service tax comes to Rs. 12200."

"But this is more than what you quoted earlier for the parts," Deepak said.

"Sir, but you are getting free parts replacement for the next 2 years as well, with this deal," Patvardhan said.

"Ok, put my wife back on the line," Deepak said.

"What do you think?" Deepak asked her.

"Well, there's that party we are hosting at home the day after tomorrow; we can't take the nuisance of installing a new RO filter now and we can't do without one either; let's take the warranty that he's offering."

"Ok then, give him the money," Deepak conceded.

"Ok, I'll go buy the parts and come," Patvardhan gave Jyoti the bill, took the money from her and stepped out.

When Patvardhan did not return for quite some time, Jyoti phoned his mobile but it was switched off.

She informed Deepak, "Hey, this fellow seems to have switched off his phone, what do I do now?"

"No worries, he'll probably come back tomorrow, maybe he didn't find the parts," Deepak was unperturbed.

But when the RO serviceman did not turn up even after 2 days, they then tried to report the matter on the complaints website.

None of the phone numbers on the bill that Patvardhan had given them seemed to be working.

Meanwhile, Jyoti dug out the old bill she had for the RO filter and found the helpline number on it.

Deepak phoned this helpline number.

"Your man has taken 12000 rupees from us and has not turned up again."

"Tell me the bill number please."

What the call-centre woman told them next was very shocking.

"Sir, there is no one by the name of Patvardhan working for us and this bill does not belong to us either. In fact, we have no records of having received any complaints from you."

It was now very obvious, they had been swindled! What was to be done now?

"We should make a police complaint about this," Jyoti suggested.

"For 12000 rupees, who's going to take the headache of constant to and fro to the police station.... let it go."

"Let's speak to Amit, maybe he could help us out."

Jyoti phoned me and related the entire incident.

"Can you send me the link on which you made the complaint?" I asked her.

"Sure, I'll look it up and send it to you right away."

"Also send me Patvardhan's number, the one he phoned you from," I further instructed her.

"Yes, sure, I must be having his number on my call register," Jyoti replied.

As soon as Jyoti sent me the link, I began to research it on Google. A few minutes of searching brought up feedback websites which had quite a list of complaints about this link- claiming it to be fake and that many people had been fooled and cheated through it. Since it wasn't a very comprehensive list, the police hadn't received any news about it yet.

I went on the DNS Look up website to find out the owner of this website.

This link was registered on a godaddy US server and there were no owner details mentioned, only an email ID.

Meanwhile I told Jyoti to lodge a complaint with the Cyber Cell.

I came to know from the Cyber cell that Patvardhan's phone is switched off from the day he took the money and his KYC details were false.

It was apparent by now that this was a cloned website; it took servicing requests of the RO Water Company and thus swindled many people.

"They must have tricked a lot of people this way," Deepak said.

"Yes, and be thankful that he just took your money; a criminal was in your house, anything could have happened."

"Oh my god," Deepak was very worried now.

I began to gather information from other people who had been similarly duped and had spoken up about it on Facebook or on the other complaint site; the numbers from which they received calls, their locations, timings, service persons names etc.

After amassing every bit of information I apped it on the internet and this is what came of it.

1. This group was most active in UP West and Delhi-NCR.

2. They always chose the timings of 2-3 pm to do their servicing.

3. Their mode of working was the same, we found around 10-12 complaints online.

4. The phones used by them were all switched off and KYC details were bogus.

Prof. Triveni Singh, who was SP STF at that time. I was with him and we were discussing this case.When people don't register a complaint with the police it only encourages such crimes to go unchecked.

The criminal is assuming that for just 10-15 thousand rupees, why the police would get on his case.

"Yes sir, but it is very important to teach such people a lesson."

"Trap them," Mr. Triveni said.

"The perpetrators are not aware that we are on to them and this web-link is still active."

"Put in at least 8-10 complaints using bogus names, they will surely contact one of them."

"Yes, that sounds like a plan," I replied with a smile.

We made around 8 complaints, citing different locations; after 2 days we had still not received a single phone call; we were beginning to think that maybe it was too late...

"Sir, somebody has made this website, we have to try and get to him somehow," I said.

"But how?" Mr. Triveni asked.

"This website is not very secure; you grant me the permission, I'll hack into it and get some data out."

"Ok, go ahead," Mr. Triveni said.

And that's how it began... a novel approach to nab a cyber criminal.

We scanned the entire website using an app security tool; we found many things lacking, because of which we could hack this website.

Using innumerable tools and scripts, after 12 hours of non-stop laboring the admin control of the website was now in my hands.

We had a well of information now.

1. The names and details of all the persons who have used this portal, till date, to register complaints.
2. Whoever created and uploaded this website.
3. Email IDs to which the data from this website was forwarded.

Upon tracking the Admin's IP we were able to successfully get his location. On further enquiring we were also able to obtain his mobile details.

As soon as we had the mobile details, we got hold of the subscriber's details. It was someone called Avinash Baghel.

WIFE'S PICTURES ON WHATSAPP

I'm not upset that you lied to me, I'm upset that from now on I can't believe you

He thought he could stay hidden behind the internet and nobody would ever catch him.

He would download pictures of women from Facebook, morph them and would turn them into nude pics. He would then send out these pics to people.

His thought process and course of actions were limited to crime programs he had watched on TV. He was under the impression that if he used a UK number to WhatsApp nobody would ever be able to trace him.

What he was not aware was that there was someone watching every move of his. If he hadn't been nabbed yet it was only because the police were trying to get enough evidence to put him away for 10 years and not just for 3 years.

It was Prashant's promotion party today and we were celebrating with our friends at a restaurant in Hauz Khas, Delhi.

Vidyut received a WhatsApp message just then; he glanced at the message and promptly hid his phone from view. His expression turned grave; it was evident that something about the message had made him uneasy.

"Ok people, I'm taking off now, I just remembered I have some important work to finish at the office," Vidyut got up to leave.

"But the party has just started and we have gotten hold of you after such a long time, stay a while longer," Prashant tried to hold on to Vidyut as he passed by him.

"No Prashant, it's really urgent," Vidyut replied a bit irritably.

Upon hearing his brusque tone no one else dared to hold him back.

"Come then, I will walk you out," I stood up to accompany him.

At the Parking lot I asked Vidyut, "Is everything alright?"

"Yes, yes, everything is fine," Vidyut answered with a nervous laugh.

Although I felt that he was hiding something it didn't seem like the right moment to ask, so I didn't press him further.

I returned to the party. Around 11:30 pm I got a call from Vidyut.

"Party over?" he asked me.

"Yes, we were just leaving," I answered.

"Come to CP once you're done, I want to discuss something important with you, don't tell anyone," Vidyut instructed me.

All the hang-outs in CP were closing soon; we couldn't get a table anywhere so we decided to sit in the parking lot.

"What's up?" I turned down the music in my car and enquired.

"Something for which I cannot approach the police for help; I was hoping you may be able to help me," Vidyut replied.

"But what has happened," I asked, concerned, placing a hand on my friend's shoulder.

"I received a WhatsApp message today," Vidyut said in a tiny voice.

"What was it about?" I turned towards him and asked.

"It contains pictures of Shruti..."

"So...?"

"Naked pictures of Shruti," he turned to me and said.

"What?" I was very taken aback.

Shruti is Vidyut's wife; she works as a Software Engineer in an IT company.

"Are you certain that it's her in the pictures?" I asked after deliberating a bit.

"I spoke to Shruti, these aren't her pics; these are morphed images. I just don't have the nerve to take these to the police."

"But Pal, if the pictures are not even of her then why worry. Anyone can morph pictures; this is how these perverts take advantage of us. In my opinion, even if such pictures are of us we must not hesitate to report it. The criminal should be the one who is afraid, not us."

"I know, but I just don't have the nerve."

"Ok, listen, the police have a women's helpline-1090, put in a complaint on this; you can make an anonymous complaint too if you so wish," I suggested.

"I have a feeling this is someone I know," Vidyut said.

"Anyone you suspect?" I asked.

"What number did the message come from?"

"It's a UK number," Vidyut replied.

"Send me the number."

"Amit...," Vidyut looked at me again.

"This wasn't the first time..."

"Around 8 months ago I had received a call from another UK number. The caller warned me that he had some private photos of my wife. I ignored the call, didn't give it any thought, but since then this man has been a menace to us. I haven't even told Shruti about this."

"But today, when I discussed this matter with Shruti I learned something even more shocking."

"What's that?"

"She too has been receiving such messages."

"Meaning...?"

"The same morphed photos."

"Did she receive the messages from the same number?" I asked.

"No, it's a different number every time but usually a UK number."

"Hmmm...he's a crafty chap; he knows how to keep his identity hidden. But don't worry we are smarter than him; he won't be able to stay hidden for long using tricks he learned through films or YouTube. Send me all the numbers he has used to communicate with you."

"I don't have all the numbers; the numbers he first contacted me from, I had blocked those numbers and subsequently deleted those messages."

"Send me whichever numbers you do have."

"Send me the message text, the sender's number, the application from which it was sent, such as Facebook, whatsApp etc."

"Also send me the sending time, which is at what time the message was sent."

"Also sending content, what was the message sent... can you figure out where this content was sourced from... was a WhatsApp profile pic used, or is it from Facebook photos or from Instagam?"

"Make a record of all this. The police will also require these details and I too will begin my investigation with the help of these details."

Vidyut gave me a list of 7 numbers through which he had received, at different times all the WhatsApp messages.

To find out more information related to these numbers, I used open source tools such as Truecaller, Twilio, Opencam, Whocallsme, Carrier look up etc.

Many of these advanced tools can tell us the location where these numbers have been active in the recent past.

According to my investigations I learned that the old numbers were now deactivated, however, the current number that was used to send the WhatsApp message was done using a WiFi network.

Of particular importance was the fact that the location of the old numbers was near Leyland area, in UK, in a town called Preston.

I also found out that the perpetrator was using an IPhone and was sending these WhatsApp messages with the help of Sky UK Limited WiFi.

I phoned a friend I have in the National Crime Agency in UK. I requested him to help me find out details of this number and the WiFi owner.

Although I did keep in mind that this criminal could be someone from India itself and was probably using UK numbers to keep his identity concealed.

It would take some time to get the information from the UK; meanwhile I continued my investigation here.

I looked through the messages carefully again. It was apparent that the criminal knew of personal details that could not be easily obtained; Vidyut was not very active on social media, hence the person responsible had to be someone close to them.

"Whoever this person is, he has done his homework well, he knows many minute details about you," I said to Vidyut.

This freaked Vidyut out even more.

"You mentioned that this chap phoned you about 8 months ago..."

"Yes...?"

"Would you be able to recognize his voice?"

"Yes...maybe..." Vidyut replied, thinking.

"Ok...then...let's begin a reverse investigation"

"What is that?" Vidyut turned towards me and asked.

"Tell me the names of all those persons that you suspect. I will collect their voice samples through a call-centre. Somebody will call each of them and will record all conversations for quality purpose," I replied with a smile.

I also looked up all these suspects on Facebook and other social media sites. I was especially looking to see if anyone had any connections in UK, a friend maybe, someone who was aiding him in this.

"Install a recorder on your phone. If he calls again, record the call. And if you get any other message, let me know instantly. That will help," I instructed Vidyut.

At my suggestion, Vidyut put in a complaint with the Cyber Cell as well. With the help of the Cyber Cell we emailed WhatsApp legal support asking for details of the device owner who had used WhatsApp from this number at so and so timings.

We also asked for the IMEI number of the device and whether any other WhatsApp number was used on this device.

We were now awaiting 3 results:

A reply from the National Crime Agency, UK.

A reply from WhatsApp Legal.

Any other message from the Perpetrator.

In the interim we also received the voice recordings from the call centre. I sent these recordings to Vidyut and asked him to listen to them carefully, over and over, to see whether any of those voices sounded like that of the anonymous caller.

By that evening, Vidyut phoned me to inform that he couldn't recognize any particular voice as that of the caller; in fact he was uncertain whether any of them was indeed the caller.

So even this exercise was of no use.

NCA and WhatsApp were taking their own sweet time.

It was a Saturday; Kumud was showing me some pictures on Facebook, "Look at this, Sonika and her family on their Europe tour."

While looking through those pics, I noticed a birthday alert for Vidyut's wife, Shruti.

I quickly went to Shruti's account and began looking through her photos. I must have hardly gone through a few pictures when something clicked in my brains.

I phoned Vidyut immediately and asked him, "I have identified a few Facebook pics of Shruti, take a look at these and tell me whether the morphed pics that you were sent- were the faces of those taken from any of these?"

I had Vidyut's reply in a short while, "Yes, the faces were used from these very pics."

"We have got our man then," I replied jubilantly.

I contacted the Cyber Cell and got them to email Facebook's legal department. I got their reply after 5 days.

I now had the criminal's IP address!

His location was Delhi itself; it was an Airtel IP, so I straight away emailed the Internet Service providers with the IP details asking for the details of the device owner.

By that evening I had the details of that crafty man.

"Dinesh Harzai. Do you know him?" I showed Vidyut his photograph and details.

"I know him! He is Shruti's colleague; I have met him a couple of times. He seemed like a decent guy... He did all this?? This is really shocking!"

"Can the police arrest him for doing this?"

"Yes, absolutely, in accordance with the IT Act this is a severe crime, punishable by law. But we shall wait a bit longer, we have all the proof we need, he has been exposed."

"But how did you find him?" Vidyut asked.

"Well, anytime we access anyone's Facebook profile or download any photo from there, Facebook keeps a record of that user."

"That day when you confirmed that it was those Facebook pics that the criminal had used to make the morphed images, I got an email sent to Facebook legal asking them for details of those persons who have accessed Shruti's Facebook page in the last month and details of the person who had downloaded these 3 pictures, in particular, from her page. Clearly the perp had directly downloaded these pics from Shruti's Facebook to create the morphed pictures."

"Facebook sent us the IP address of the criminal and with the help of that we got his device details his mobile number."

"Wow, this is absolutely amazing work," Vidyut was very pleased.

After about 10 days we received responses from NCA, WhatsApp and Instagram. From the IP address and device ID it was now confirmed that it was Dinesh Harzai who had been harassing Shruti and Vidyut for the last 8 months.

The police made out cases against sections 66C, 66D, 66E and 67A of the IT Act and arrested Dinesh Harzai. A lot of evidence was collected from his mobile and laptop as well; he had morphed images of other women as well.

He is now in jail.

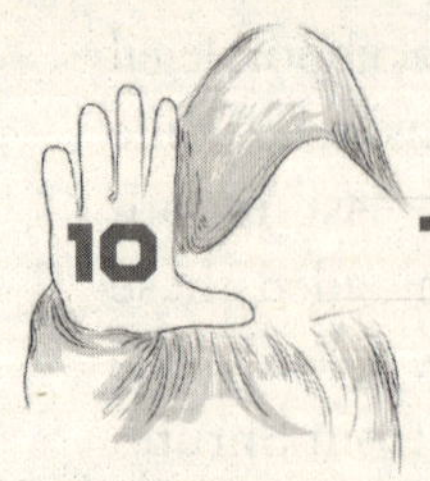

10 THE STRANGE WORLD

Conversations are happening whether you are there or not

It was a cold, wintry Sunday morning and not even 6 am when Kumud woke me up by pulling at my blanket.

"Get up, you have to go for a run today," Kumud's not-so-sweet tone soon had me wide awake.

We have a running group whose members are AT, Robin, Krishan, Chhaya, RKM, Seema, Manisha, MK, Preeti and many more and they are all crazy runners. I am the laziest of them all and today there was a plan to run 8-10 kilometres.

I just washed my face, put on my shoes, thought for a while and picked up my mobile phone as well.

"Arrey did you see that video yesterda", AT said while running.

"Its shocking, How can somebody do that?", Krishan ji responded.

"That was a fake video. It was morphed." Before anyone could say anything else, I had put a full stop on the conversation.

"How do you know that it was fake?" Preeti asked.

"Ask Seema, she will confirm it. After all she's a journalist."

Seema responded by saying that– A little bit of googling can reveal that it was fake.

It must have been around 6:45am and I was totally drenched with sweat when I received a call on my phone.

It was a call from Khushbu Jain. Such an early morning call. This was not normal.

Khushbu Jain is a renowned Supreme Court Lawyer.

"Sorry to bother you early morning, but I need some help," Khushbu said.

"What happened?" I thought it must be something serious.

There is a case of 67. (Circulation of unlawful or obscene material) of Information Technology Act.

"Yes, but what happened?"

"There has been offensive content circulation oversome WhatsApp group, against which a group member has complained and Police has arrested the Whatsapp group admin. Moreover the admin is not even getting bail".

"Ok, so how can I help in this case?"

"I think my client is not guilty. He has not done anything wrong. But we need clear evidence which can prove his innocence."

"What was the offensive content"– I asked.

"Some hate content, against a religion."

"What makes you think that your client is innocent, I asked."

"I have dealt with many criminals and victims, I have seen clever people. I can sense whether the person is saying the truth or not." Khushbu said.

I trusted Khushbu's instinct.

"Ok, send me your client's social media handles, and also send me the details of the group in which these hate messages have been sent. I will also need one more mobile phone number from that group." I said

"Ok, I will send you," Khushbu said.

In some time I had all the social media handles of a person named Anubhav Prakash.

Through a social media analytics tool, I did some sentiment analysis of this person. These kind of tools help in understanding the mentality of a person to quite an extent. The qualities such as depression, irritation, anger etc can be judged through these tools. We can also know if the person often tries to hurt someone or is a balanced guy. What are his political inclinations etc.

Through Social Media analysis, it was clear that Anubhav's reactions have never been too aggressive or harsh. He seemed to be a person with a balanced opinion.

I called up Khushbu.

"I think you are right. His Social Media Sentiments analysis says that he is a balanced personality but still I would like to meet him."

Next day Khushbu and I went to meet Anubhav in prison.

"Was this message sent by mistake through your account?" I asked Anubhav.

"I have not sent this message," Anubhav clearly specified.

"So, was your phone with someone else when this message was sent?"

"No, it was with me only."

"Then how come this message was sent?"

"I have no idea about the same."

"Do you think your phone has been hacked?"

"Why would anyone hack my phone sir, I am a very ordinary man."

"Do you know of any suspect who might be wanting to take some revenge or any person who might be wanting to harm you?"

"I can't recall any such thing." Anubhav said after thinking for some time.

After talking to Anubhav, one thing was clear that he didn't know much about the incident, which meant that either he was being trapped or he has done something by mistake but we needed evidence to prove this.

"Is Anubhav's phone with the police?" I asked Khushbu.

"Yes, they have seized it and they are analyzing it. Who is the investigating officer?" I asked Inspector.

"Veer Singh," Khushbu replied.

We will have to talk to the investigating officer once. May be we get some clue from his findings.

When we reached the police station and talked to the investigating officer, he said– "Message has been sent from his phone only. We have clear evidence for that and the FIR is against him."

"Can we get a copy of the analysis report of the phone or can we get the cloned copy of the data"– I requested.

"We can't give you the data but our team is working on the cloned data so if you wish, you can see the cloned data here only"- Veer Singh ji replied.

Through Digital forensics the original phone is preserved as it is and a cloned copy is prepared so that all the investigation happens over the cloned copy and the original remains intact. The Original data has to be preserved and a hash key is crated for it. Hash key is a unique signature of any memory. This is to make sure and prove in the court that the original data has not been tampered. The court can ask this to be verified any time, on demand basis.

The investigation then happens on the cloned copy and if there is any tampering, anywhere, then the hash key gets changed.

I started analyzing the cloned data and was looking at the communication of all WhatsApp groups I noticed that there was a WhatsApp group by the name "Funny World", which had all its members with foreign numbers, mostly UK, Bangladesh and Pakistani numbers.

Apart from that there was one more surprising thing that all the links which were forwarded on that group, did not have any content now. This was not normal. This is something like that I send you one news from a newspaper link today and the next day, the news is deleted from that website.

Fortunately, apart from that one hate video message, there was no unusual activity in any of the WhatsApp groups of Anubhav.

I noted down all the phone numbers of that group "Funny World", took some more data from the phone and I asked Khushbu to set up one more meeting with Anubhav.

When we met Anubhav the next day, I asked him– "Why does your WhatsApp group– Funny World has so many UK, Bangladeshi and Pakistani numbers? Do you know all of them?"

"No Sir, I don't know any of them".

"Then why did you add them in this WhatsApp group?"

"I didn't add them, they added me." Anubhav said.

"What are you saying, you are the only group admin of that group, so the numbers must have been added by you only."

"No sir, how can I be the only group admin? I have never added any number"– He seemed pretty shocked.

"You don't know any of the group members, you are the group admin, you did not add any of those numbers, then how did you reach the group"– I was a little irritated.

"Sir, this happens many times. Someone adds you to an unknown group and moreover when I was added to this group, its name was not "Funny world."

What! I was a little surprised, then what was its name?

"The strange world", Anubhav replied.

"I noticed many times that I was added to some unknown groups. Usually, I exit them immediately but this time the name of the group sounded quite interesting so I thought let me see what kind of posts come on the group, and I will exit if they don't interest me.

There were some cult practices discussed on the group Out of curiosity I started reading those posts and following those links and sometimes I even forwarded one or two links that I liked."

"The strange world", sounds interesting.

"Yes sir, I also thought that this is some international research group and that is why I did not exit it."

When I started analyzing all the international numbers of the group, the story started unfolding.

Anubhav was a victim of Cross border social media influencer group.

"What does that mean?", Khushbu looked at me and asked.

These days many countries use this technique to create influence among the public of neighbouring countries. This is something like what Cambridge Analytica did through Facebook.

The same thing happens over a WhatsApp network also and it happens with a lot of planning.

1. They first create a WhatsApp group which has all international numbers.
2. Then they source numbers of some people from neighbouring countries and add them to the group.
3. If you don't quit the group soon, then you become their target. They try to add more people through your network and they also try to get themselves added to your other groups.
4. Sometimes, they embed the group invite in the message that they send on the group.
5. You think that you are forwarding some interesting image or video but it's actually a group invite which you accidentally send to your friends.
6. Whosoever accesses those forwarded images or videos, he also becomes a group member. Though mostly people will exit the group immediately, but some people don't care and accidentally remain a part of the group.

8. Through that whatsapp group, they easily hack the person's mobile as well.
9. Sometimes they even blackmail you.
10. At first, there is normal content shared on the group, so that the people don't quit but soon after these kind of groups are used to make a content viral.

Anubhav is still in a better situation because due to the hate video, fortunately there were no riots or any mis-happenings, but if that is the case, then within the IT acts, you shall not be spared.

The biggest learning from this case was that we should not randomly become a part of any group, we should be watchful before clicking any link and we should be very careful as to who is the admin of the group. If the admin is not known, you should immediately quit the group, because the group admin can any day make you the admin and exit the group safely, you might not even notice this. Moreover, we should never forward any link without being sure of its content.

If a group has more than one admin or if all the people of a group are admin, then there are many simple techniques, by which any unknown man can become a part of that group and once he becomes a part of the group, then using a little bit of trick, he can even become the group admin and control the group.

Anubhav had become a victim of all these techniques. Fortunately his forward did not turn violent, so we could manage to get him out of this mess.

11 ONLINE EMPLOYMENT

I will always choose a lazy person to do a difficult job because he will find an easy way to do it

This incident occurred about three years ago. It was summer time and I was extremely busy those days. I was headed to the cafeteria for lunch when I got a call..

It was Akash on the line. Akash was an HR Head of a very large Multi National Company, JW Software. He sounded very worried.

"A thousand people have suddenly turned up atmy company office today to join work. There is absolute confusion." He said.

"What is the confusion for; your company must have called them in right?"

"No, that's just it; my company did not call them," I was taken aback, "What are you saying?"

"Yes, we didn't release these offer letters; somebody has issued more than a thousand of these fake letters in our company's name."

"Goodness, who could have done this?"

"It's really not a simple matter, when we told these people that we hadn't released these offers there was absolute pandemonium; some people started breaking furniture; it appears that someone has taken money from these people in exchange for the offer letters."

"That's crazy, have you informed the police?"

"Yes, I have just informed the local police and they are sending a team here. But I think this a case of Cyber fraud, which is why I thought of calling you."

"Ok, I'm on my way." and I left for sector 62 without having lunch.

When I reached there I saw an angry mob outside, shouting and heckling; nobody was ready to listen to reason. The police were not letting anybody in.

I looked around, I noticed a young man sitting in a corner, and he appeared to be crying. I walked up to him and asked, "What's your name?"

"He looked up at me and after a moment's hesitation replied, "Rajesh Sharma."

There were tears in his eyes.

"What happened, tell me..." I asked him.

"What difference will it make sir," a few more tears rolled down his cheeks. He appeared really broken up.

"Maybe I can help you," I tried to appease him.

"How would you do that? Can you get me a job?" he asked in the same polite tone as mine.

"I don't know about a job... but I can help catch the person who has deceived you."

"It makes no difference now, people always take advantage of a person in a sad state and there is no worse situation to be in than that of being unemployed."

"At least if we catch him he won't be able to do this to others," I replied.

Rajesh took out a file from his bag and handed it to me.

The file contained a lot of printed out email communication and an offer letter.

Rajesh began recounting his tale, "About 3 months ago I received an email from an HR firm called Signature Recruitment. They claimed to be a recruitment firm and were conducting a collective recruitment for some MNCs."

"When they mentioned JW Software I was immediately interested and expressed my wish to appear for an interview."

"In their next email they asked me to pay 7000 rupees."

"On asking what for, they said that it was an interview processing fee."

"I paid them the money."

"How did you make the payment?" I asked.

"Through PAYTM."

"After that I went through two rounds of Technical interviews, that went off quite well."

"I was following up almost every day. Two days later I received a mail saying that I had been selected."

"And ten days after that I received an offer letter from JW Software. The email ID was that of JW Software so I wasn't in the least suspicious."

"That was a spoof email; by spoofing emails you can use anyone's email ID to send a mail," I explained to him.

"I don't know about this bhaiya." Rajesh looked at me and said.

"Then what happened?" I asked.

"What was surprising was that they gave me a joining date for 6 months later. But I was very relieved that I had a job now. I threw a party for some of my friends at a restaurant and informed all my relatives that I had got a job with JW Software. It was the best time of my life."

"Then about 15 days ago I received a call from the recruitment agency. They informed me that the company requires some employees to start work urgently; they said they could arrange for my joining date to be moved forward."

"I did want to start working soon, so that I could financially help out at home."

"So I told the recruitment agency to go ahead."

"They said that they will need to pay some money to the JW Software HR to join earlier."

"I asked them how much."

"They said Rs. 55000."

"55000 was a big amount for me, I suggested they deduct it from my salary as I could not arrange for this amount so quickly."

"But they would not agree to this, they said they needed the money before I joined otherwise they could give the joining date to some other candidate."

"So I somehow managed to borrow 55000 rupees and transferred it to the recruitment firm."

"And so I set off from home today, as it is my joining date. It was the best morning of my life. My father even bought me new shoes," Rajesh gestured towards his shoes as he spoke.

Overhearing our conversation some more candidates were now gathered around us; some more of them began to narrate their accounts.

I held Rajesh by both his shoulders, pulled him up and gave him a tight hug.

"You all have been duped; if you wish the perpetrator to be caught then I will need all of your help."

"Yes, we are ready to help," quite a few of them answered.

"Please make a list of all the email IDs and numbers that were used to contact you all; and please make another list of your names and numbers so that I can get in touch with you."

Meanwhile, Inspector Rahul had also joined us and he began to make a note of people's complaints.

When the police checked out the bank account where all these people had transferred their money to, they found that most of the money had already been withdrawn from different ATMs and the rest had been transferred to a bank account in Hyderabad. We got the

KYC details of that bank account and paid a visit to the account holder's home. It turned out to be the home of a rickshaw driver. He appeared scared to see the police at his door.

"Is this your bank account?" the police asked him.

"No sir, it's not," the rickshaw driver was scared and close to tears.

"Then why is your Aadhar card linked to it?"

"Sir I had loaned out my Aadhar card, for Rs. 500 per month."

"What are you saying, you lent your Aadhar card?" the police were baffled. How could anyone loan out their Aadhar card?

The rickshaw driver continued his story, "They gave me Rs. 2000 and said that they need to open a bank account for a year using my Aadhar. And that accordingly they will pay me Rs. 4000 more."

"Who were these people? Do you have their names, addresses or phone numbers?"

"No sir, they always came to my house, they appear to be educated young men."

"When did they last come to your house?"

"Two months ago sir."

"Have they borrowed anyone else's Aadhar card?"

"I don't know sir."

"Ok, if they visit you again, let us know immediately."

"Yes sir, Inspector sir."

All the phone numbers used by the perpetrators were now switched off. Our targets had already gone underground. The KYC details of all the numbers were that of rickshaw drivers and labourers; the SIM cards had been generated in the names of these labourers etc.

The website of Signature Recruitment had been hosted from a US site and we could not obtain any clear KYC details of it except for a Gmail ID. This Gmail ID however, would be very useful to me.

I immediately, sent Google support a 91 CRPC request, asking for all the login IPs, secondary emails and Meta data details associated with this ID.

I began analyzing all the names used in mail communication on the open web to see if I could find any job posts related to them. But I found nothing.

By checking the old locations of the SIM cards we did get to know that these people were operating from around Meerut and Delhi; but they had not used these numbers for any communication other than contacting the candidates.

We were not able to get any leads; not through call data records, not through social media and neither through open web analysis.

Just then Mr. Triveni phoned me.

“What are you stuck with?”

“Arrey sir, the case I discussed with you yesterday has got me stumped. God knows how many people have been swindled by these men.”

“How did they take the money?” Mr. Triveni asked.

"Mostly through PAYTM."

"Have you analyzed all the transactions?"

"Yes, according to the details we have, most of the money was received via PAYTM, only one transfer was made to a Hyderabad account but the KYC details of that are false."

"Maybe there have been some other payments made at some time?"

"It doesn't appear so."

"Analyze the details once more, maybe you missed something," Mr. Triveni suggested.

The next day, once again, I asked for the PAYTM wallet transaction details of all the numbers, going back 6 months.

I had the transaction details by that evening.

I began looking through every transaction one by one. PAYTM was used mostly to receive the money.

There were no payments done through them.

Suddenly I noticed one transaction in particular.

Mr. Triveni's instinct had been right; this PAYTM wallet had been used to recharge a pre-paid mobile number. I noted down the number, it was a Vodafone number.

I looked up the number on truecaller; it belonged to a woman named Sadhna. I dialled the number, it was ringing, and this meant that the number was active. Bingo! I slammed my hand on the table and right away phoned Inspector Prakash.

"Locate this number and put the address under surveillance, this will unravel everything."

The number belonged to an address in a village near Meerut. When the police turned up and interrogated Sadhna, she spilled everything.

Sadhna's boyfriend, Ajay, was the mastermind behind all this.

When the police finally nabbed Ajay, a lot more shocking details came to the surface. Ajay had used around 10 major Indian companies' names to commit fraud, but these other cases never reached the ears of the police as the swindled amount was not too big and the number of people duped were also few.

He tried to go for big game this time and was exposed.

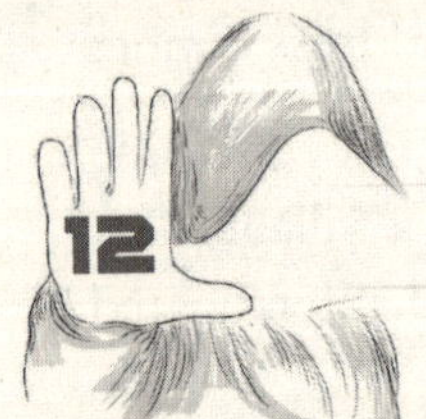

12 THE CYBER GROOM

The true identity theft is not financial. It's not in cyberspace. It's spiritual. It's been taken

This was around 3 years ago, I was working at my laptop when Kumud reminded me, "Don't take on any engagements on the 10th, it is Preeti's ring ceremony on that day."

"Oh yes, thanks for reminding me; what's the name of the boy and what does he do?"

"Abhaas Shukla; he's an IRS officer, from a very good family. His mother too was in a senior government post, she has retired now; and his father is also a retired IAS officer. He seems to be a really nice guy; Preeti is absolutely crazy about him, she can't stop singing his praises."

"Ya, men are always nice," I smiled and said.

"Yes, it was just my bad luck that I ended up with you," Kumud taunted.

Before I could come up with a reply, Kumud received a phone call.

"Hi Preeti... what's up?" Kumud said.

"What!!??" It appeared from Kumud's reaction that something was wrong.

"Here, talk to Amit."

"Hello Preeti, what happened," I took the phone from Kumud.

"Bhaiya, I just received a call from the Mumbai Police, they were asking me about someone called Prateek Saxena."

"Do you know this person?"

"No, I don't know him, but actually Abhaas asked me to transfer 10 lakhs into Prateek Saxena's account."

"What for?"

"Well, we are booking a flat in Mumbai, so this was the booking amount for that."

"Ok, but why do you sound worried, what did the police say?"

"They asked me why I had transferred the money to this person. I told them that I had done so because my fiancé Abhaas had told me to, it was an advance to book a flat."

"Ok, so what is it that's distressing you?"

"They told me that this Prateek Saxena is not a builder and neither is he a resident of Mumbai."

"Really?" I was surprised.

"I then tried phoning Abhaas but I couldn't reach him," Preeti continued.

"Don't worry, he's probably busy, I'm sure he'll ring you back."

"No, this is very unusual, his phone his switched off, I just spoke to him this morning," Preeti said. "Ok, what can I do?"

"Please could you find out through your contacts with Mumbai Police what exactly the matter is?"

"Alright, send me the number from which you received the call."

I phoned the number and found out what the matter really was about; what I was told by the police astounded me.

The Inspector told me that a woman had lodged a complaint of fraud against this Prateek Saxena.

Prateek had scammed her of the amount of Rs. 55 lakhs. When the police investigated Prateek's account, they found 17 lakhs transferred to him from a Preeti Shrivastav, which was why they had phoned Preeti.

I immediately had the impression that something was very wrong here. I asked the inspector, "Do you have a picture of Prateek Saxena?"

"Yes, we do," the inspector said.

"Could you please WhatsApp it to me, I have a feeling that I can help you on this case."

The inspector sent me the picture, I showed it to Kumud; we were both stunned.

"This is Abhaas," Preeti had sent us a picture of Abhaas; it was evident that Prateek and Abhaas were the same person.

I began a Google search of Abhaas's photo using certain open source analysis tools.

However I found nothing related to him; this was weird in itself, his not having a Facebook or a LinkedIn profile in today's day and age.

To learn anything further I needed to speak with Preeti, but in person, not over the phone.

"Invite Preeti over, I need to sit her down and have a chat with her," I said to Kumud.

That evening, Preeti was at our home, sitting in front of us.

When Kumud told her about Abhaas and Prateek being one and the same person she was dumb founded; she just could not believe that Abhaas could possibly have deceived her.

"Did you give him 17 lakh rupees?"

"Yes, I transferred him money 3 times."

"But why on earth would you do that," I asked irritably.

Preeti burst into loud sobs.

"Ok, tell me everything from the beginning; how did you meet Abhaas; who else knows him?" I tried to ask calmly.

After a while, her sobs subsided and she began telling me her story.

"I met Abhaas through bharatmatrimony.com."

"He contacted me first. I liked his profile so we exchanged numbers and began speaking to each other. He told me everything about himself and his parents; that he was an IRS officer and that his parents were retired civil servants."

"Did you ever speak to his parents?" I stopped her narration mid-way to enquire.

"No, a couple of times my parents did say that they wished to speak to his parents, but he said that they were travelling most of the time so we never did get to speak with them."

"When did he meet you?"

"About 3 months ago; he said he was coming to Delhi and would like to meet me; I met him at Hotel Le Meridian."

"And then...?"

"He was really impressive. I liked him very much; he was exactly the kind of man I had been looking for, I was so happy that I had found someone like him."

"He would send me gifts almost every week. We were speaking over the phone almost every day; we began to plan a future together."

"He told me that he was planning to buy a flat in Mumbai and that after we were married, we would live there. He sent me pictures of the apartment. It costed 2 crores and there was a down payment of 30 lakhs for it. He said he would need my help to pay the down payment but after that the EMI would be his responsibility alone."

"And that's why you transferred 17 lakhs into his account..."

"Not to his account... he sent me details of Prateek Saxena's account... My entire savings..." and Preeti dissolved into tears once more.

"Preeti, Prateek Saxena and Abhaas are the same person, you have to admit you can see that now..."

"I want this man caught, at any cost," Preeti's eyes were red with anger now.

"Were you not suspicious when you saw that he didn't have Facebook or LinkedIn profiles?"

"He told me that he was an undercover officer and that he wasn't allowed to have any social media profiles," Preeti replied.

"Besides his mobile number and account number, what other details do you have of him?" I asked.

"I have his ID card and his passport."

"Are those in Abhaas's name?"

"Yes, he told me that he is in the midst of investigating a sensitive case and that some people are after him; somebody tried to snatch his bag when he was in Delhi. So before he left he handed over his organization's ID card and passport to me for safe keeping."

"Bring me these documents tomorrow morning, I will, meanwhile, continue to trace him."

I phoned inspector Khanwalkar of the Mumbai Police once again and informed him that Prateek Saxena had duped Preeti Shrivastav using the alias Abhaas.

The inspector told me that a woman named Revti, from Mumbai had lodged a complaint against Prateek Saxena; he had taken 24 lakhs from her and had promised to marry her but disappeared soon after taking the money. The two had met on shaadi.com.

Inspector Khanwalkar further informed me that Prateek Saxena's bank account was registered to a Bangalore address. A team of police officers had been sent to that address where they met a woman called Ramya who claimed that Prateek Saxena was her husband.

"What!?"

"Yes, they got married just 4 months ago. According to Ramya, Prateek has been living in Mumbai as his job is there. At first, upon learningof Prateek's doings she was completely taken aback. She wasn't ready to believe that Prateek could have done something like this. But when we shared all the details with her and showed her photos of Prateek and Revti together, she agreed to help us. Now she may also file a case against him."

The story was unfolding quickly. It was apparent that this man, Prateek Saxena had fooled a number of women; but what was his real identity... this remained a mystery so far.

"We have got 4 different phone numbers for him so far; all 4 are registered with fake KYC details.Please help us trace this man," the inspector requested me.

"Put in a request on 91 CRPC; his profile is on bharatmatrimony.com or shaadi.com, access those."

"Through this we will come to know all the women he has gotten in touch with. Also, find out from these websites what account he used to make the website payments and what is the access IP address of it."

"Send me all the details that you unearth."

"Also find the complete CDR details of these 4 numbers, he must definitely have, at some point or the other, used one of these numbers to call someone he knew personally."

"We are analyzing the CDR sir," the inspector said.

The next morning Preeti brought me Abhaas's ID card and passport.

"They appear absolutely genuine," I looked at them carefully, turning them over.

"His ID has his office address; did you ever ring his office to find out more about him?"

"No, because it's a Delhi address on the ID."

When I enquired at the CBDT office, I learned that, there was, indeed, a person by the name of Abhaas employed there. He was posted abroad. It was becoming evident that this Prateek Saxena had done his planning thoroughly. He knew that the CBDT Dept. had an IRS officer by the name of Abhaas and he took full advantage of this knowledge to make out his entire game-plan.

I was deep in thought, wondering how to find this elusive Prateek Saxena a.k.a Abhaas when I received a call from the inspector.

"Sir, upon CDR analysis we have a list of about 15 women whom Prateek has duped using a different name every time."

"Hmmm.... this list could be even longer... let's wait for Prateek's account access details from the matrimonial sites."

The next day we had received the account details of Prateek and Abhaas from the matrimonial sites. After analyzing everything it was obvious that this man was exceedingly devious. He had duped 25-30 women so far. But where and how had he disappeared into thin air?

I said to the inspector, “Why has this fellow suddenly disappeared, how did he come to know that the police is on his tail, he would have phoned Preeti or someone if not.”

“I think he hasn’t really disappeared, I think this is his usual strategy; once he gets the money he goes missing and it is quite possible that at this very moment he is looking out for a new prey, using a totally new identity.”

“May I get the list of numbers of the women he has conned? I would like to speak with them; I may find a clue through them.”

The inspector sent me the list. After speaking to many of these women this was what I learned: Prateek is around 30-31 years old.

He speaks English very well. He doesn’t understand certain Hindi words and often asks the meanings of those.

He has an in depth knowledge of Bengali literature and often quoted Bengali writers when he wanted to impress anyone.

Some women also noticed that he spoke mostly with a Bengali accent.

He had excellent knowledge about Taxation and tax laws, he had often rightly advised people relating to this.

He claimed his hobbies were music and tennis.

The weirdest thing of all was that he had told all the women that his parents names were Pratibha and Devesh, but using different surnames every time.

With the help of this information I began to look for him on all possible matrimonial sites. The most important key right now were the names of his parents. I soon found many profiles with Prateek's a.k.a Abhaas's picture, but with different names in each. Most of these profiles were not active anymore but I did find one active profile on shaadi.com in the name of Shailesh.

Using his profile access we learned that he was in touch with a woman named Tanya at the moment; she was in Gujarat. We had also been successful in obtaining his current mobile number.

The mobile was put under surveillance; it was showing his location to be Kolkata. The phone was switched off most of the time, it would be switched on once in a while when he was speaking to Tanya.

Police teams traced his location to a particular area in Kolkata. They began showing his photo and asking the people in that area whether anyone knew him or recognized him. The security guard of one society identified him as 'Anirban Das'. When the police knocked on Anirban Das's door his wife did not open the door. From a neighbour, the police got another phone number for Anirban Das and also a number of his wife's. This was unmistakably Anirban's a.k.a Prateek's a.k.a Abhaas's real number.

After a lot of labour and legwork Anirban was finally caught. It was then that a lot more came to light. Anirban Das was a married man, he even had a child. His wife and family were also involved in all his many deceptions and swindles.

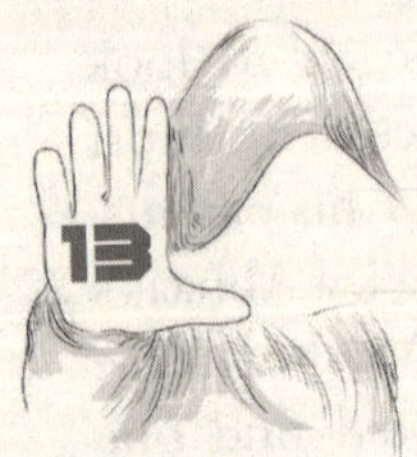

DARKWEB-SILKROAD

Money often costs too much

Before I begin this story, I would like to share some interesting facts with you. In today's day and age if you want to find something or if you are looking for any kind of information, it just takes you a few seconds, thanks to Google. If you want info about a person or if you need to confirm certain facts, Google has the answer to it all, everything is available on the internet.

But what if I were to tell you that the portion of internet that you can actually access via Google is just a fraction- just 4% or even lesser is what we are actually accessing.

That's right, 96% of the internet is not accessible via Google. To enter this special world of the internet you require special tools. This inner, secret world of the internet is known as DarkWeb or DeepWeb.

The DarkWeb contains the world's shadiest crimes. Here you can buy stolen IDs, stolen credit/debit cards, any kind of narcotic and any kind of weapon. Here you can hire goons and also buy any kind of ID proof such as Driving licenses, Passports and even Aadhar cards.

This story is about this deep, dark world.

It was December 2018, the atmosphere was festive all around, and people were getting ready to ring in the New Year.

"Where do you plan to celebrate New Year's Eve this year?" Mr. Kukreja asked me; we were out for an evening stroll in the society.

"Like always, at home; we go to bed early," I replied smiling at him.

"Come on, we should go somewhere and party," he laughed out.

"Let's see... if I don't have any prior engagements then why not... we can surely party," I replied.

"Oh to hell with work, you work all the time, what kind of a life is this anyway?"

Mr. Kukreja was right. What kind of a life was this? I really was working too much. Not this time, I told myself. To hell with work, this New Years Eve I would party hard.

"Ok sir, you're on. I'm available to party. Bye-bye work."

And we both burst out laughing.

Still laughing, I turned towards home, just then I got a phone call from the IG, "There's a meeting scheduled for tomorrow, I would like you to join us as well."

It occurred to me that this was a conspiracy to ruin my New Year's Eve party plans but I couldn't really refuse the IG, so I turned up at the designated time of the meeting, the next morning.

The meeting was concerning certain special measures to be taken for New Year's Eve.

The IG was speaking, "Every year, just before New Year's Eve there is a big supply of illegal drugs in India. The majority of these are weed, cannabis wax, cocaine, hashish etc."

"This year as well, we have received information, that these drugs are going to be supplied at many secret New Year parties. We have aggressively checked everything out but we have been unable to find a single clue."

"There are numerous drug peddlers, but the channels used to bring these drugs into India-that is what we need to find out."

"Have you looked into DarkWeb?" I asked.

"What is that?" ACP Rajendra Singh asked.

"All illegal activities take place through the DarkWeb these days," I replied.

"It's very possible that these peddlers are ordering the drugs using the DarkWeb."

"But everything on the DarkWeb is anonymous isn't it? It will be very difficult to figure out where these people are actually sitting and making these deals from." SP Anant said.

"Difficult yes, but not impossible," I replied.

"Order and payment on DarkWeb may be anonymous but for deliveries they must be using The Awakening couriers or standard post."

"The first thing to do is to scan international couriers very thoroughly."

"We are very vigilant about scanning them yet somehow these parcels seem to get through," the SP said.

"Let's analyse this market."

I began to analyze e-commerce portals on DarkWeb especially portals like SilkRoad and DreamMarket.

First I scrutinized the addresses of the crypto currency wallets to see which wallets had made payments in the last month. When we had identified certain wallet addresses we cross referenced them with every Indian exchange in the hope of getting more details about the wallet owners.

A lot of time and energy was spent on this exercise but we were unable to come up with any clues.

The IG phoned me on 22nd December, "Did you find anything on the DarkWeb?"

"No sir, although we have been trying our best."

"Is there any means for us to enter the system and get to them that way?" the IG suggested.

"There is only one way to do that," I replied thoughtfully.

"What way?" the IG asked immediately.

"We can enter the DarkWeb network by posing as a buyer and supplier."

"The anonymity of the DarkWeb will work in our favour."

"And for this I will require permission."

"Fine... keep me informed and involved at every step though," the IG acceded.

After that we registered on all the popular ecommerce websites on DarkWeb using different IDs for vendor registrations and buyer registrations. We must have made over 60 registrations but no E-commerce Portal was accepting us as a vendor or as a buyer.

On researching DarkWeb further I learned that new users on DarkWeb could enter only on the recommendation of verified users. To conceal themselves from the eyes of the police the vendor selection process had very tight security measures.

We reduced our rates, gave quality assurance commitments, offered local delivery options and tried many other ways to entice them but even after 10 days of trials we had not managed any breakthroughs.

"This process may take a very long time," the SP said.

"I agree with you sir, I think we should offer them something exclusive, something that nobody else has."

"What could that be?"

"Something different... something very dangerous..."

I looked into a very rare drug and posted something related to it. This wasn't a total waste; some foreigners began contacting us but we were still waiting for an Indian to take our bait.

Almost all the vendors on DarkWeb had a rating. I analyzed all the registered vendors carefully and noticed that there were some feedbacks from Indians as well. I made a note of all the handle names of the Indian feedback. Nobody used their real names on DarkWeb, they all used pseudonames to make their deals.

I found names such as 'Toyworld', 'RegalDog', 'LightofAsia', 'Kohinoor', 'Fakkad' etc.

I then analyzed these names on the open web, especially on ecommerce sites. But this wasn't as easy as it sounds. There were fleeting chances of success in what I was trying to do.

After a lot of searching and data analysis I was finally able to get my teeth on something. A pseudo-name that I had got from DarkWeb's SilkRoad website also turned up on the open web on an eBay portal. Someone had used 'Kohinoor' as a pseudo-name to leave feedback on a toy. I now had to trace the location of this name.

This was not so difficult. I sent EBay a 91 CRPC request, asking for this customer's IP with time stamp.

EBay replied in a few days with the IP address.

We sent these IP details along with the time stamps to Airtel and after 3 more days they sent us the address of the Wi-Fi owner who had accessed this Wi-Fi at the time.

But this was not enough, this person could be someone else altogether. Besides, it was not a crime to use a pseudo-name to leave a feedback on a toy like product. We could not take any action at this point; we still needed to find a bigger confirmation or evidence.

The address was of Peetampura area. We notified all of Delhi's international courier companies and instructed them to inform the police immediately if any national/international couriers were to come to this address.

We were still trying to get close to any verified vendor on DarkWeb but we were not succeeding.

Just then we received a call from Bluedart courier services. "Sir, there is a delivery to be made at the address you told us about; international package of toys, the parcel is from California."

A break... finally!

"How big is the parcel?"

"Sir, around 9kgs, they are toys."

"How is the delivery going to be made?"

"We contacted the receiver sir; he has to pay some taxes on the parcel, so he said he would collect it from our offices."

"At what time is he expected?"

"Tomorrow morning between 9 and 10."

On 31st December at 8:30 am, police officers in plain clothes were at the Bluedart office; alert and on the lookout.

It was now 9:45 am and nobody had turned up yet to claim the parcel. Just then, a big Honda City car with VIP license plates pulled up at the entrance to the Bluedart office.

The police were watching; there were two young men inside the car, they appeared to be in their early twenties. One was behind the wheel and the other got out and entered the Bluedart office.

The police immediately received a call alert from the Bluedart office; this was the person come to pick up the package.

The man walked out of the office and was just placing the package in the boot of the car when. The police surrounded the car. Both men were arrested.

The package was opened, it contained toys within a special airtight packing. On breaking the toys, a white powder poured out of them. We had caught our peddlers!

So friends, this was the story and through this story the one message I want to give you is that no matter what the technology and no matter how much anonymity an online tool claims, if you commit a crime you cannot hide it for long. Just like in real life, you are constantly leaving behind thousands of footprints or clues unknowingly; someone may have seen you, someone may have heard your voice, your fingerprints... similarly there are footprints one leaves behind in the virtual world as well. No crime is perfect.

The case was hence solved and just in time too, it was 31st and time to party!

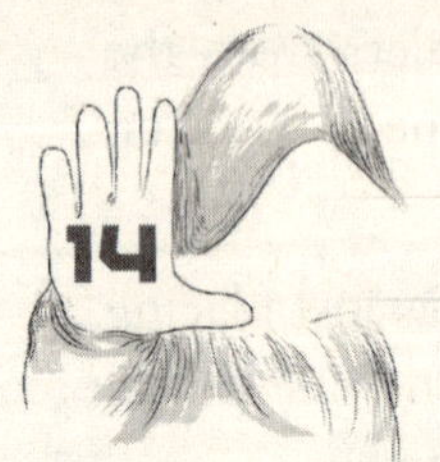

14 THE CAT'S MURDER

The score never interested me, only the game

I was with SHO Pratap that day, when a constable came and announced, "Sir that man has come, the one about the cat."

"About a cat?" I asked, surprised.

SHO Pratap replied, "Arrey, this is a really strange complaint that has come and I am being pressured to deal with it as it involves a retired judge."

"What exactly is the complaint?" I asked.

"Someone threw his cat off the roof of his building."

I was astonished, "Threw a cat off the roof? But why would someone do such a thing to an innocent animal?"

"The owners of the cat have complained that it was done by their neighbours, before this incident too, they have had arguments regarding the cat. Now they feel that this extreme step was definitely taken by their neighbours."

"Have you spoken to these neighbours?"

"Yes, we did inquire but these people are not going to accept that they have done it. And we don't have any proof against them either. There's no CCTV there and no witnesses. What can we do really? So, I have called this neighbour in today."

"Can I also meet him and have a chat with him?" I asked.

"Arrey Amit ji, this is not a Cyber crime case, it's not something you would understand, let it be."

"But I am very curious to meet this person who could have harmed an innocent animal just out of anger."

"Ok fine, sit, I'll call him in."

In a little while, Aditya Melhotra was seated in front of us. He was a sober looking man and appeared to be around 35-40 years of age.

"All fingers seem to be pointing to you Mr. Aditya, now you tell me, how can we not think it's you who has done this," the officer said.

"Come now sir, how can you possibly believe what these people are saying? They are extremely quarrelsome, always picking up a fight about something or the other and it's always about something trivial."

"How often did you quarrel regarding the cat?"

"Just the one time, their cat had somehow gotten into our house; we were unaware about this, so we locked the house and stepped out for an errand. By the time we returned, the cat had created a big mess all over our house. So we explained to them politely and told them to keep a better eye on their cat."

"You mentioned that they often pick up fights, if you fought regarding the cat only one time then what were the other fights about?" I intervened.

"About completely petty matters; one day they came over to ours and accused us of having siphoned the petrol out of their vehicle. Now you tell me, why on earth would I steal the petrol from their vehicle?"

"So had the petrol actually been siphoned out of their vehicle?"

"Now, how would I know that? I think these people are just constantly looking for excuses to pick up a fight."

"Yes, but, Aditya ji, they would not fling their cat off the roof just to find an excuse to pick a fight with you, would they? Tell me, do they quarrel with anyone else or just you?"

Aditya Melhotra had no answer to this.

"See, the cat was flung from the roof just above your flat, you were home that day, and you have had disagreements regarding the cat in the past; this makes it apparent to me that you must have done this," the SHO now appeared strict as he said this.

"Come on sir, that terrace is open to everybody, it's the society's roof, I am not the only one accessing it; besides what will I get by killing their cat," Aditya's voice shook a little as he replied.

"I don't know anything about this and we hardly use the terrace."

"If you didn't do it then someone must have, right? Who else goes to the terrace?"

"Some of the society workers go and children play there often."

"Ok, what other matters did you have a quarrel about, with Mr. Puri, anything else that's weird?" I interrupted once more, to ask.

"Sir, everything has been weird of late."

"The other day he picked up a fight with me saying that I had set fire to his bed sheet, the one he had hung out to dry on the roof."

This sounded really strange. "Give me a written list of all the things you both have quarreled over in the last 2-3 months."

Aditya immediately picked up a pen and paper and began writing out a list. After that the SHO told him to leave.

"Don't you think this is a strange list... stealing petrol, burning bed sheets, throwing stones andnow the cat..." I asked.

SHO Pratap nodded in agreement, "Do you think it's some phantom force?" he whispered.

"Even ghosts are afraid of the police, why are you getting scared officer?" I laughed and replied.

"Oh well... what should I do now...?" SHO Pratap stood wondering.

"I think we should go and speak to Mr. Puri as well. This appears to be a really strange state of affairs."

"Right then, let's go pay him a visit at his residence. We may get a better feel of the situation there too."

It being a Sunday, it was my day off, so I readily agreed.

It was 2 in the afternoon when we reached Mr. Puri's home. This was a society with low-rise buildings; Mr. Puri lived on the second floor and Mr. Melhotra was on the top floor, that is, the fourth floor. There was a lock on the door of the third floor flat, nobody was living there.

Mr. Puri's household comprised of him, his wife and their 9 year old grandson.

"We heard that someone had set fire to your bed sheets," I began the conversation.

"Arrey, these people are always looking for ways to annoy us, that bed sheet was drying on the roof and the water from it was dripping onto their balcony so I'm quite certain that they only set fire to it."

"And your petrol too had been stolen some time ago...?"

"Yes, around two weeks ago."

"From which vehicle?"

"I have got a Scooty for making short runs to the markets nearby, the petrol was taken from it."

"How did you come to know that your petrol had been stolen?"

"The scooter just would not start, when I checked I saw that there was no petrol in it."

It was during this time that I noticed Mr. Puri's grandson, he was totally engrossed, playing a game on his mobile phone. He did not look up from it even once, as we sat there talking.

"Is this your grandson?"

"Yes."

"What is your name beta?"

"Ayaan, answer him," Mr. Puri said, a bit sternly.

"Namaste uncle," Ayaan looked up, greeted us and then got absorbed into his game again.

"Which game are you playing?"

Ayaan did not reply.

"Is it PUBG?" I smiled and asked.

"PUBG is for kids, I don't play PUBG," Ayaan replied dryly.

Mr. Puri sensed Ayaan's tone and said, "These children nowadays are into their mobile phones all the time, no matter how much I try to explain to him he doesn't listen. His mom goes off to work and his dad is in Dubai, and he just doesn't listen to us." Mr. Puri was ranting now.

"Mr. Puri, the incidents related by Mr. Melhotra sound very strange- petrol being siphoned out, bed sheets set on fire and now this thing about your cat... tell me, have there been more such weird incidents that appeared unusual to you?"

"No, I don't recall any other unusual incidents."

Just then Mrs. Puri came from the kitchen and said,"Arrey, tell them about that time... goodness, it really scared me."

"Why, what happened?" I asked, reaching for the cup of coffee.

"Arrey, I woke up at 2 am one night and I noticed the stove was on in the kitchen although we had all gone to bed. I was terrified; goodness knows how long the stove had been left on; I shouted and woke everyone up. But everyone seemed to think that I only must have left the stove on, but I distinctly remember switching it off before I went to bed."

SHO Pratap glanced towards me.

"Is there a full-time maid working here?" Pratap asked.

"No sir, my maid leaves at 6 pm"

"Hmmm.... ok, we will continue with our investigations, if we find something we will let you know."

Pratap and I left their house and we were walking towards our car when we noticed some children playing in the grounds downstairs. I called out to one of the children.

"Yes, uncle?" the child asked me.

"Do you know Ayaan?"

"Yes."

"Is he your friend?"

"No, he is not our friend, he is a champion."

"Champion of what?

"Of mobile gaming; he always scores better than us in any game."

"What are your thoughts?" Pratap asked me.

"What did you think about Ayaan?" I asked him back.

"He's a strange boy I felt, doesn't speak much; maybe his parents don't get along... there is definitely something strange about that family."

"Yes, I too felt the same," I said.

When I reached home, I Googled all these strange incidents- stealing of petrol, burning bed sheets, the stove being lit at night.. I found a lot of information, there are many mobile games that present these challenges to the players asking them to fulfill these. But I could not find the link to any of these games. It appeared that the link to such games was available only on recommendation or by winning a different game.

I phoned Pratap, "The clue to all these incidents lies in the phone that Ayaan was playing on, we need to go pay them a visit again tomorrow and check out that mobile phone."

Ayaan was at school when we reached Mr. Puri's house the next day.

"Can we have a look at that phone please, the one Ayaan was playing his game on, yesterday?"

"Yes certainly, it's my phone," Mr. Puri unplugged it from the charger and handed it to me.

I took the phone and began to scroll through it; there were many games on it.

I analyzed every game one by one and then one particular game caught my attention.

The game was called 'George Challenge'.

When I tried launching the game it asked me to enter a password.

I wasn't able to enter the game.

There was no sharing option in this game either so I could not even copy it to my phone.

"Do you know anything about this game?" I asked Mr. Puri.

"Which game?" he asked, glancing at the screen.

"George Challenge."

"No, I have never noticed it," he said.

"It is password protected," I told him.

"Really?" Mr. Puri again stared at the game in my hand.

"Can you tell me what the password could be?"

"I have no idea; Ayaan must have put in this game."

"I would like to try cracking this password if I have your permission to do so; we feel that this game holds the answers to a lot of what we are seeking."

"Yes, yes, of course, please go ahead," Mr. Puri nodded in assent but he appeared completely baffled.

I connected the mobile phone to my laptop, launched ADB and attempted a brute force attack of a combination of passwords on it.

We sat around drinking coffee...

About 30 minutes later there was a pop-up on my laptop-Brute force successful. We had cracked the password.

I began exploring each level of the game one by one and the mystery began unraveling.

"Did Ayaan ever hurt his right hand, something like a cut made by a blade?" I asked, while glancing into the mobile screen.

"Yes, yes he did. How did you know?" he asked surprised.

"Have you ever lost some money too?"

"No, I don't think I ever lost money," Mr. Puri said, thinking.

"Try to remember... you may have lost it on 27th September."

"Yes, yes, I remember... I thought maybe I had misplaced it," Mrs. Puri suddenly chimed in.

"7500 rupees?"

"Yes, exactly 7500 rupees!"

"And the petrol from your scooter was stolen on 8th October."

"Yes!" Mr. and Mrs. Puri were both looking at me now, completely bewildered.

"Your bed sheet was set on fire on 17th October."

"Yes!" Now SHO Pratap and the Puris were looking at me with wide-eyed wonder.

"I am very sorry to tell you this Mr. Puri but your cat was killed by Ayaan."

Mr. and Mrs. Puri sat there stunned!

"But why?" he asked.

"It is part of a game; he's at the 8th stage now."

I wasn't able to see the next stage of the game; that would be revealed only when the current step had concluded.

We were sitting there worried, deep in thought when Ayaan came into the room.

Mrs. Puri was just about to start scolding him when I gestured her to say nothing.

He flinched, involuntarily, when he saw us there.

"Hello Ayaan, we need your help with something."

"What kind of help?" Ayaan approached us and sat down near us.

"We are developing a game; I heard that you are a mobile game champion, so I require some feedback about a game."

"Feedback for what?"

"For George Challenge." I said.

Ayaan flinched again and then glared at us angrily.

"We have come to know via the gaming community that you have crossed the 8th stage."

"You are lying," Ayaan shouted.

"No... no, we are not lying," Pratap said.

"You are lying," Ayaan again shouted and then ran towards his room.

We were shaken for a moment and then we raced after him.

Ayaan had shut himself into his room. I was very afraid.

"What did we lie about, at least tell me that," I shouted from outside the closed door.

"You lied about two things," Ayaan shouted back.

"What two lies?" I asked.

"You people are not here to get any feedback for a game," he yelled.

"And what is the other lie," I asked, very scared now.

"I am not on the 8th but on the 10th step," Ayaan said.

OH MY GOD! "Break down the door, quick!" I yelled at Pratap.

We began hitting and shoving the door, hard.

"Hurry up, hurry up, break it down," I was terrified now. Nobody could understand what was happening.

All of a sudden, the door jamb broke, Ayaan was lying there unconscious.

We rushed him to a hospital.

Ayaan's life was saved... but this game had put a fear in my heart forever.

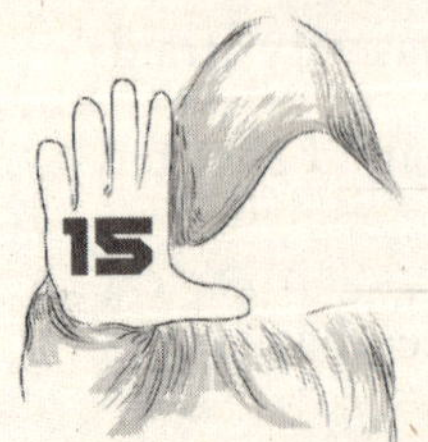

15 HONEY-MONEY

Every lie is two lies, the lie we tell others and the lie we tell ourselves to justify it.

This incident occurred sometime in August 2016, I was in London attending a Hackers conference. I was approached by some Pakistani app developers; they showed me a secure chat messenger app which really impressed me.

Time went by, as it's wont to do; about 6 months after that conference, I received a call from my friend Preetesh. Preetesh is a reporter for a very popular News Channel.

He sounded afraid.

He said, "Tell me something; how can I find out if my phone has been hacked?"

"Why, what happened; why would someone hack your phone?" I asked, surprised.

"No... I just feel there's something wrong," Preetesh answered hesitatingly.

"But why do you feel this way?"

"I can't mention over the phone; can you tell me of a simple trick so I can find out whether it is true?"

"Yes, there is a trick but it would be better if I could personally analyze your phone."

"Ok then, but meet me outside; let's meet this evening at the Café Coffee Day near ITO."

I reached the coffee shop that evening at the decided hour. Preetesh was already there, waiting for me.

He began to speak as soon as I sat down.

"You have to keep this to yourself."

I gestured with my eyes that he could trust me with that.

He began to recount his tale, "A few months ago I got a friend request from a girl called Damini. From her profile it appeared that she was a journalist and that she worked for the Indian Defence News portal; we had some common friends as well, mostly in the army and police services."

"As soon as I accepted her request I got a message from her."

'Jai Hind'

"I replied back- 'Jai hind'."

"Her Facebook wall had a very attractive picture of her, smiling while saluting the Indian flag. Therewas even an Indian Defence News logo on a banner. Everything was very impressive."

She asked me, "Are you posted somewhere in Delhi?"

I replied, "Yes."

Then she wrote, "So are you in Power Corridors?"

I replied, "Yes, indeed."

We used to chat on and off on ordinary topics. Then, one day, I got a message from her.

'Preetesh, there's something important I need to discuss about,'

'I have received a piece of information which may be of use to you.'

"It was about some recent infantry movement of Pakistan in association with some Chinese training. I found the information interesting and so I wrote a piece about it and the information turned out to be accurate," Preetesh said.

I asked her, "Where did you get this info from, your network appears to be superb."

She replied, "A friend, just like you, helped me get it."

"About 8-10 days after, I received another message from her."

'There is something important I have to share but it's not safe for me to do so on WhatsApp, I will send you a secure chat messenger, we can use this for our private communication,'

"She sent me the link and I installed that app."

"From then on we would chat only using that application."

"She sent me lots of interesting pieces of information, mostly to do with Chinese and Pakistani activities."

"Then she phoned me one day."

"Was it a voice call?" I asked.

"Yes, on the same messenger app."

"We spoke for about 30-40 minutes; the topics ranged from Indian history to political systems."

"She was really nice; her voice was sweet as honey."

"Hmmm.... and then?" I continued looking at him as he spoke.

"Then one day she messaged me saying that she has a friend in the UK who wanted to write an article about the Indian Air force; basically to cover the strength of Indian Defence. She asked whether I could help out her friend with that."

"What kind of information was she asking for?" I asked.

"Like what are the different army bases in India, their strength etc.," Preetesh replied.

"Then... ?"

"I Googled some information and gave it to her."

"But I began to feel something was wrong when she requested something very odd; she sent me the co-ordinates of some air-bases and asked me whether I could send her photographs of these locations."

"I told her, how can I give you these?"

"Damini replied, you are in the defence, can't you even do this much?"

"That is when I thought that there was some misunderstanding; this girl had taken me to be someone else."

"Why did you think so?"

In reply, Preetesh showed me his mobile screen. "Have you seen my profile pic?"

On his Facebook profile pic, Preetesh was in a soldier's uniform.

As soon as I saw the pic I understood what was up, "She thinks you are a soldier in the army."

Preetesh continued, "I absolutely refused to help her with any of this kind of information."

"But I was stunned when she sent me a particular audio clip."

"What was on the audio clip?" I asked, my eyes widening.

"It was a recording of a conversation I had with another woman."

"What kind of recording?" my eyes bored into him.

"It's something that I wouldn't want the world to know about. I don't know how Damini got it but she is now blackmailing me with it."

"I think something is wrong with my phone, I'm pretty sure it's been hacked and I don't know what other recordings of my conversations she has. This is why I am so afraid and I think you can help me with this."

"Hand me your phone," I asked Preetesh.

Preetesh's hands shook as he pulled out a phone from his bag. "Here you are; I switched this off as soon as I got suspicious and I have also removed the SIM card and put it into a new phone. This one is the one I used to talk to that woman, I have a feeling it was recording all my conversations."

I turned the phone over to find out which make and model it was. Preetesh had gone very pale now.

He folded his palms and imploringly asked me again, "I can trust you, right?"

I grasped his folded palms and said, "Don't worry, I am not going to switch this on now, I will get home and then investigate it and you will lose none of your data."

"Also, give me Damini's Facebook profile and also the one of that girl from London."

I switched on my laptop and began analyzing the Facebook profiles.

"Both these profiles have been generated from the same IP," I turned my laptop screen towards Preetesh.

"Where are these IPs from?" Preetesh asked.

I looked up the location of the IPs on ip2location.com and we were both knocked for a six at the result before us. Google map showed a location in Karachi, which was near an army base in Pakistan.

What !!?

We both were now convinced that Preetesh had fallen prey to a case of honey-trapping.

"Have you ever shared any sensitive information with her?"

"No, I have only shared what is already available on Google."

"I have a bad feeling that this is part of a bigger conspiracy, if I could fall prey to this scheme then there must be others too; army officers too maybe. I really think something big is being planned, we need to inform the police right away." Preetesh said.

"Yes, certainly, we should inform the police. However to get to the root of this matter I think it's very important for you to continue being in connection with this woman. Keep chatting with her and I will tell you how to proceed from here."

"But what if she sends those recordings of me to someone," Preetesh asked nervously.

"Don't worry about that. She won't do anything of that sort because that won't be of any use to her. She's using that only as an advantage to scare you; so you continue with the pretence now and only do what she asks you to do."

"What are you saying; how can I do what she asks me to?"

"I'll tell you how."

On reaching home, I began analyzing the Facebook profiles of those girls; and one after another shocking facts came to light.

70-80% of their friends were from either the Indian Defence forces or the Indian police while the login location of the girls was Karachi.

The Anti Terrorist Squad had taken my information very seriously and they were already working on this.

I began profiling all the army officers from the friends list of these girls; where they were from, what was the nature of their jobs etc. We found around 780 profiles out of which at least 540 were on sensitive job postings.

I analyzed the cell phone Preetesh gave me; I used reverse engineering on the chat application that Damini had asked him to install and my findings had alarm bells ringing in my mind.

This wasn't just a chat app; it was a surveillance app; almost all the content of Preetesh's phone was being transmitted to somewhere else- images, videos, texts as well as any conversations.

This may be the reason why that woman knew everything about Preetesh, including his shortcomings. She was making her moves very cleverly.

I said to the SP of the Anti-Terrorist Squad, "Sir, our main problem is how to do damage control with this predicament; it is very obvious that there are more people behind this and not just this one woman."

"We need to do something that will completely break down their network; they definitely have a lot of lines connecting them to India," the SP replied.

I said to Preetesh, "Can you somehow get that woman to come and meet you in Delhi? Tell her that you can provide her with the information she wants but that you are uncomfortable with sending soft copies; it would be better if she collected it from you on a pen-drive."

"But how will she come to Delhi when we know very well that she is in Karachi?" Preetesh asked.

"That's exactly it; you know that she is in Karachi but she is not aware that you know that. She has told you that her location is Jalandhar so obviously it's normal if you should call her to Delhi. What we need to see is whether she is so tempted by the offer of information that she sends someone in place of herself. And if she does send someone, that person will help us find out just how far- reaching their network is in India." I replied.

"Ok, I will try..." said Preetesh.

Meanwhile the ATS had made contact with the departments of those 540 people and were keeping an eye on their activities but it wasn't as simple as that; we could not suspect everyone. Yet, there could be someone amongst these, who was unwittingly caught in this web and could cause serious harm to India's security.

It is not a crime to make friends on Facebook using a fake profile; we needed more obvious evidence.

I was also gathering open source intelligence on those Facebook IDs in the meantime.

There were no other social media connections to those IDs, like LinkedIn, Instagram or Twitter. This made it evident that these Facebook IDs had been created for a particular purpose.

We were in a fix, trying to figure out how we could get more information when I received a message from Preetesh- 'We need to meet.'

On meeting Preetesh he told me that the girl was ready to meet with him.

The SP and I were energized with this bit of news.

The place for the rendezvous was decided upon- a restaurant in Khan Market at 5 pm.

Preetesh conveyed the place and time to Damini.

Plain clothes policemen were deployed to that area from very early in the morning.

CCTV cameras were being used to keep a sharp look-out at every person going in and out of there.

At 4:30 pm, Preetesh was seated alone at a reserved table in the restaurant.

We were keeping an eye on Preetesh through the cameras installed in the restaurant.

We were waiting... tense... our heart rates escalating. Just then we noticed a woman walking towards the restaurant; she moved with quick steps and entered the restaurant. All the officers were in position; we had no clue as to what she was capable of doing.

She hurried up to the reception counter, spoke with the person there for a moment and just as quickly left the restaurant.

We called the person sitting at the reception counter in, to ask what had transpired, but he said that she had just been enquiring about booking a venue for a party.

Nothing was happening, the clock now showed that it was past 5:30, Preetesh had already consumed a few cups of coffee whilst waiting but nobody turned up.

At 5:40 Preetesh phoned Damini from that same app but there was no answer. Damini was not responding.

Around 6:10 Preetesh came running out of the restaurant; we were standing near where our car was parked, he came straight towards us. Beads of sweat were collecting on his forehead, he showed us his mobile screen; there was a message from Damini. 'This will be avenged... do you really think the police are smarter than us?'

Seeing this, sweat broke out on our foreheads too. How could this information have been leaked? This operation was known to just a few chosen people.

Now we were suspicious of every person who was on this case with us. One of them could have also fallen prey to this honey-trapping and may be getting blackmailed right this very minute.

It was now imperative to find out who else had become a victim of this honey-trap and was sending out sensitive information about India.

"Did this woman ever phone you from any other number; any mobile number?" I asked Preetesh.

"No, I don't have any phone numbers for her but I do have a number for her friend from London; I had once received a call from that- +4589899." Preetesh replied.

We were clutching at straws now so I was grateful to have at least that number to work with.

But it was also possible that this number too may be virtual and we might not be able to get to this woman just by that number alone. In the meantime a lot of our moves had already been exposed.

I looked at the number and said, "Let's try reverse phishing."

"What's that?" almost everyone asked me.

"We will use this UK number to send messages to all 540 suspects; let's find out who knows her really well."

By SMS spoofing we sent out messages to every possible suspect.

All we wrote was- 'Hello.'

Most did not reply to it, one or two replied with a 'Hello.'

But Shobit Kumar, an officer with the BSF wrote: 'Hello Neha, how are you?'

Shobit was obviously familiar with this number.

We called Shobit in for an enquiry. Through talks with him we came to know a lot more about this case, but unfortunately, it being very sensitive information, I cannot share the details of it with you, the reader.

16 ONLINE CAR SALE

The world is one big data problem

Imagine that you gave your phone to someone else for one hour in a day; and that with the help of technology I can tell you exactly, that at so-and-so time, your phone was with someone else. How would that make you feel? What I am trying to say is that if a person gives his phone to someone else for some time to prove that he was at some other location when the crime was committed, he still won't be able to avoid being caught.

This story will tell you about just such an incident and how I did this and why I did this.

It was a Friday morning and I was already looking forward to the weekend when I received a call from Tanmay.

"Hey, I have a colleague, Rajesh Asthana and he has been missing since last evening, can you find out his location please?"

"Missing...what do you mean missing... have you made a complaint to the police?" I asked surprised.

"Yes, I have registered a complaint with the police."

"Give me the name of the Investigation Officer, I will speak to him and see."

I had just hung up with Tanmay when I received a call from Abhishek Pandey; he was the CEO of a company in Bangalore.

"There's a man missing from the society I live in, since last evening."

"Rajesh Asthana?" I asked immediately.

"Yes. Yes... but how did you know?"

"Someone just called me about the same."

"Oh... Ok."

"I'm just about to speak with the IO."

"All right, thanks, please do your best," Abhishek said.

I thought I would eat my breakfast and would then speak with the IO at length. I sat down at the dining table.

I had barely eaten one bite when I received a call from Sanjay. Sanjay is a political leader.

He too asked me to help locate Rajesh Asthana.

This was really strange; within half an hour I had received calls from three different people requesting me to help locate this Rajesh Asthana.

I understood that the matter was of grave importance.

I telephoned the IO immediately.

I introduced myself and asked him whether he was the one investigating Rajesh Asthana's case.

"Yes sir," Inspector Murugan replied.

"What information have you got so far?"

"Sir, Rajesh Asthana is a software engineer and he has been missing since last evening. His phone was switched off at 10:25 pm last night and his last location was M.G Road. This is all the information we have. He left his home at 5 pm yesterday in his i20 car."

"Who all did he last speak to?" I asked.

"Sir, I have the numbers of all those he spoke to last. One is his brother, two are friends and one is an unknown number. He has spoken with this unknown number five times but this number is also switched off now; we are currently trying to find out the customer details (KYC) of this number.

"Ok, did Rajesh mention anything in his conversations... like where he was planning to go?"

"No sir, he didn't mention anything of the sort, he spoke for a very short time and that too on some technical subject."

"Ok, send me that unknown number; I too am investigating this case so if you find any local clues please do let me know," I said.

"Ok sir," Murugan replied.

I phoned Tanmay next and asked him for some details, "Please send me all of Rajesh's social media handles and his Gmail ID as well."

In a short while, I had all the social media handles and I began analyzing them.

I found some posts on Rajesh's Facebook profile; I could probably get some clues from this. If there was anything particular going on in Rajesh's mind I could find out through Facebook.

In the meantime I got a call from Murugan, "Sir, the KYC of that unknown number turned out to be false."

"Ok then, at least get the call details of that number," I said.

"Yes sir, we did; other than Rajesh, that number has been used to call just two individuals and they are both cab drivers."

This meant that this person with the unknown number was our main suspect. He must be the one behind all this and he probably bought this SIM just to talk to Rajesh.

It was apparent now- Rajesh was in danger.

From those cab drivers we did get one clue; the criminal had booked the taxi using a mobile app.

We asked the mobile app based cab booking company for a record of his entire trip.

I also suggested they take the help of those cab drivers to try and generate a sketch of the person with the unknown number.

In this high-tech day and age, a software engineer had now been missing for over 24 hours.

The taxi booking company sent us the trip details of this unknown number; this cab was booked for a location in RT Nagar to Bannerghatta Road, but both these locations were restaurants.

On enquiring at the restaurants, one of the waiters at the Bannerghatta Road restaurant recognized Rajesh's photograph. He said that Rajesh was met by two people and their talk was something to do regarding buying a car.

This was a big clue for us. Rajesh had gone to sell his car.

I phoned Tanmay immediately; he and Rajesh worked in the same office.

I asked Tanmay, "At the office did Rajesh work on his laptop or at a desktop computer?"

Tanmay said he that he used to work at a desktop computer.

"Is it possible to unlock his PC?" I asked.

"Yes, with special approval our system admin can do so," Tanmay replied.

"In that case please take an approval, switch on his system and provide me with remote access to it.".

Being a sensitive case, it didn't take Tanmay very long to get an approval and soon I had Rajesh's desktop screen in front of me.

Just as I suspected, Rajesh's Gmail was open on his browser.

And with the help of this I could easily access the Google dashboard data.

At this point I should tell you that Google keeps a record of every activity of yours: every location you are at, every site you browse or search and every action of your mobile activity.

And it is very simple to access all of these.

According to his SIM card, Rajesh's last location was MG Road and after that his phone had been switched off. But Google had the information of every step he took before this. Google could tell where all he had been before and what all he did; how many times he accessed WhatsApp and what other apps there were on his phone. Everything!

After analyzing his entire location map this is what I learned:

Rajesh left his home in RT Nagar at around 5:05 pm the previous evening. He took the route through Infantry Road to reach HP Petrol Pump Bharati Service Station.

He was here for about 7 minutes so he must have filled petrol at the bunk.

From here he went to the Empire Restaurant on Bannerghatta Road; he was there for about 35 minutes.

Then he drove to a place near Shantinagar where he stopped for about 3 minutes and then continued on to Shivajinagar.

At around 9:40 he again went from there to MG Road. His phone was switched off at MG Road and there was no location for him available after this.

I sat staring at this data from Google dashboard when I finally noticed a pattern here.

Between leaving his home at 5:05pm and reaching the petrol bunk, Rajesh had checked his WhatsApp 5 times, that is, in spite of being behind the wheel.

Between the Petrol bunk and Bannerghatta Road he had checked his WhatsApp 3 times and Facebook 1 time.

Between Bannerghatta and Shantinagar he checked WhatsApp twice and again twice between Shantinagar and Shivajinagar.

But between Shivajinagar and MG Road there had been no mobile activity at all.

This made me suspect, that it was between Shivajinagar and MG Road that something had happened.

I suspected that his phone certainly travelled from Shivajinagar to MG Road but not him. Rajesh probably was to be found at the Shivajinagar location.

I phoned Inspector Murugan, "Sir, I am sending you a Google location; please look into this area and tell me what is here."

Murugan rang me back in about an hour.

"Sir, are you sure this is the right location?" Murugan asked.

"Yes, why, what is there in that place?"

"It appears to be a car garage and there is a sewer running beside it."

"You will definitely find something here, his car was halted here for quite some time; keep looking. If my analysis is right then Rajesh was taken out of the car here and someone else took his phone anddrove his car to MG Road from here," I said.

The police sternly questioned the men at the garage in Shivajinagar. They then learned that two of the garage employees had been missing since the night before, but there was still no sign of Rajesh.

We managed to get the mobile numbers of those missing men and luckily for us, one of those numbers was still on. We located the number in Mysore and the men were found and taken into custody.

The information that emerged after interrogation left our minds reeling! It was amazing how an online e-commerce portal was used to devise this crime.

Rajesh wanted to sell his car so he used this popular app on which one could buy or sell any used items, including cars. He priced his second-hand car at Rupees 3 lakhs on the app.

On seeing his offer, the criminals got in touch with Rajesh and offered him a better deal. They told him that they would give him Rupees 3,25,000 for his car but in cash only and they asked Rajesh to come to the Bannerghatta location to collect the money.

They gave Rajesh Rupees 50,000 and said that the remaining amount they had kept at their home. They went with Rajesh in his car to go collect it. They made him drive to a deserted construction site in Shantinagar. Rajesh probably refused to get down from his car so then they made him drive to the Shivajinagar garage. They murdered Rajesh there, put his body in the car and then drove to Mysore via MG Road. They switched off Rajesh's phone on MG Road, smashed it and threw it in a dustbin there.

We could not save Rajesh's life in time. But there have been many cases reported of people losing lakhs of money through such buying-selling apps. People assume that they are dealing with trustworthy buyers or sellers through these apps.

But, in truth, the app providers hold no responsibility for the honesty or sincerity of the app users and thus one could stand to lose a lot of money this way.